Tilly Beany
Saves the World

Also by Annie Dalton

The Real Tilly Beany
Commended for the Carnegie Medal
Tilly Beany and the Best Friend Machine

The Afterdark Princess
Winner of the Nottingham Oak Award
Swan Sister
Shortlisted for the Sheffield Children's Book Award
The Witch Rose

For older readers

The Alpha Box
Naming the Dark
Shortlisted for the Sheffield Children's Book Award
Night Maze
Shortlisted for the Carnegie Medal
Out of the Ordinary

ANNIE DALTON

Tilly Beany
Saves the World

illustrated by
LESLEY HARKER

mammoth

First published in Great Britain in 1997
by Mammoth, an imprint of Reed International Books Ltd
Michelin House, 81 Fulham Road, London SW3 6RB
and Auckland, Melbourne, Singapore and Toronto

Text copyright © 1997 Annie Dalton
Illustrations copyright © 1997 Lesley Harker

ISBN 0 7497 2917 1

10 9 8 7 6 5 4 3 2 1

A CIP catalogue record for this book
is available from the British Library

Printed in Great Britain by Cox & Wyman Ltd,
Reading, Berkshire

This book is for my daughter Maria who found the original dolphin stone, my daughter Anna who helped me out with the hole in the sky and for Michael Cooke for his story about the ackee tree.

Also for Jessica, for Alexander who painted the Butterfly Prince, for Sophie, Maya and Asha, for Rae and Ricardo, Tanisha, Leoni and Ricardo, and Krystal.

Thanks, too, to Kevin Nelson.

Contents

1 The hole in the sky

'Next week we're having an exciting visitor to our school,' Miss Hinchin told her class at pack-away time.

'A little bit exciting like a clown from a circus, do you mean?' asked Tilly Beany cautiously. 'Or really exciting, like a space alien.'

Tilly had noticed that teachers got excited about the oddest things. Once it was just that old road safety film!

But Miss Hinchin was fussing over missing scissors now, so instead of answering she only said, 'Wait and see, Tilly, dear,' in the warning voice she often used for Tilly.

'A space alien at this school,' giggled Bernice. 'Did you think he'd fly here in his space ship, Tilly?'

Tilly put her nose in the air. 'Anything's possible,' she said. Her mum sometimes said that.

'Where would he park?' asked Anil at once. 'In the playground?'

'He wouldn't park it, stupid,' said Joe. 'He'd leave it hovering. Then he'd come shimmering down the steps –'

'No, he wouldn't shimmer, Joe,' interrupted Tilly. 'He'd walk exactly like earth people do. And he'd –'

Miss Hinchin found the scissors. 'What an imagination, Tilly,' she said crossly. Now Tilly had

got the class thinking about space aliens, an ordinary human visitor was going to seem really boring.

She tried again. 'A writer and illustrator is coming into our class to talk about his books,' she told the children. 'His name is Mike Ryan and I'm going to read one of his books to you.' She held it up. 'It's called *The Hole in the Sky* and it's about the things that are happening to our *environment*. Does everyone know what that means? Bernice ?'

But Tilly put her fingers in her ears right away. She knew about the environment already, thanks. Her sister Sophie had pictures of seals and whales on her bedroom wall, and she never stopped going on about what cruel people did to them.

Probably Sophie would like Tilly better if she was a baby seal instead of an ordinary little girl with brown hair and bashed up knees. But Tilly didn't have a seal costume in her dressing-up box only a bear one. Anyway she'd promised to be ordinary Tilly Beany most of the time, even though there were hundreds more exciting people and things to be. She didn't mind being Tilly so much these days though, since the Beanys had moved into their new house and there were Emily, Nessa and Beth to play with after school.

Bernice's mouth had stopped moving. Tilly uncovered her ears. She didn't want to miss the story by mistake.

The book in Miss Hinchin's hands was so bright and new, Tilly wanted to sniff the pages. But the story inside was too much like the things on Sophie's wall. The humans had torn an enormous hole in the sky, as carelessly as Tilly once tore one of Mum's sheets.

Part of the sky is made of stuff called the ozone layer and that's what the hole was made in. Humans weren't looking after the forests properly, that's why the sky hole happened, so the weather went wrong. Bits of the world that were meant to stay frozen started melting, and that made the sea go wrong as well. Then all the earth's creatures got sad and ill.

Tilly wanted to block up her ears again, but she had to know what happened. She could see the other children felt the same. Stephanie's mouth kept opening like a goldfish's and forgetting to close. Adam was biting his nails and scowling. The

new twins, Leena and Beena, pushed their chairs together and twiddled each other's long, dark hair round their fingers for comfort. Beena sometimes talked to the other children in her soft little voice, but Leena only ever talked to Beena. That's why everyone called them the Quiet Twin and the Silent Twin. Miss Hinchin said Leena would talk when she was ready.

At the end of the story the animals built an ark, an animals' ark, made from bits of rubbish the humans had dumped, not the wooden Noah kind.

Then, singing a sad, sad song, they sailed the ark up through space and out through the hole in the sky, to a distant world where there were no humans to spoil things.

Tilly had never heard such a dreadful story in her life. The minute Miss Hinchin let them out of the classroom, she tore across the playground to where her mum had parked the car, threw herself on the back seat and burst into tears.

'What ever's wrong?' asked her mum.

'Drive quickly, Mum,' sobbed Tilly.

She cried the whole way home. What if Spike

had sailed away through the hole in the sky with the other animals?

But when her mum opened the kitchen door, Tilly's little cat was curled up safely in the ironing basket, making the washing gritty the way he always did. Tilly hugged him so hard he squeaked.

'Don't fly away, Spike,' she told him. 'We'll mend that old hole. Cross my heart.' Then she kissed the place on his nose that was exactly like Kate's lovely new suede boots, and took him into the kitchen and poured extra cat biscuits in his saucer to take his mind off the ozone layer.

To cheer Tilly up, Mum promised Emily could help with the Friday shopping. She could even stay for tea. But at the last minute Sophie said she was coming too. Before Tilly could say a word, her big sister marched out to the car, climbed into the front passenger seat and that was that.

'Some sisters aren't fun,' Tilly whispered to Emily. 'That's the problem. Specially the prickly kind aren't.'

Emily nodded. 'Kate isn't prickly, is she?' she whispered back.

The Beany family was like the puzzle Tilly had once, where the pieces slid into place as easily as if they were buttered. Except for the stable door which never would go in, no matter how Tilly pushed and grumbled. Sophie was like that stable door piece. She was the prickliest, most impossible girl that was ever invented.

But even with scowly old Sophie tagging along Tilly still enjoyed the drive to the supermarket. She liked it when Mum wound down her window to take the parking ticket sticking out like a dog's laughing tongue. She even liked pushing the empty trolley, giving it secret twirls, the way her brother Tom had shown her, so it waltzed like a circus pony. Most of all Tilly liked choosing the kinds of cereal and ice-cream she liked best. (The chocolate kind for both.)

Mouldy Sophie didn't enjoy choosing things, Tilly thought, so much as stopping other people choosing.

'You're not the boss of the biscuits, you know,' Tilly muttered darkly as Sophie put a packet of lovely ones back on the shelf just because they had animal fat in them.

Tilly wished Sophie wasn't vegetarian. Eating vegetables seemed to make her big sister crosser than ever. Probably Sophie didn't even like vegetables. Every week she'd bully Mum into cooking them for her, then push them round her plate while everyone else munched shepherd's pie. That's why Sophie came shopping, Tilly decided. To make sure Mum didn't buy anything nice for anyone else.

'She's a mean old shopping policewoman,' she whispered to Emily. Emily didn't have any big sisters, just one little brother called Ben. She didn't know how terrible life could be.

It wouldn't be so bad if Sophie only got angry about animal fat things. But she got angry about everything. Mum wasn't allowed to put one single thing in the trolley until Sophie read the label that said where it came from. If it was somewhere they were cutting down trees she wouldn't let Mum buy it. It was the same with toilet paper. You couldn't have the pink kind, you had to have white, and you couldn't have the flower-smelling stuff that made your clothes fluffy, because Sophie said it got into rivers and poisoned the fish.

Tilly knew Sophie was fibbing about that. The Beanys' washing-machine water went gurgling

9

into the drain in the yard. You could see it because when the drain got clogged up with bits of cabbage and rice, the soapy water spilled over the edges and wandered around on the cobbles before it soaked into the cracks. It didn't go near any rivers.

Doing the shopping Sophie's way took ages. To cheer herself up, Tilly started a game of hide and seek with Emily, but Mum told them to stop before she'd finished counting to ten. 'I don't want to go searching the supermarket for you when it's time to go,' she said.

'If you're tired,' said Tilly in her softest voice, 'what if me and Emily run around bringing you things and you just stay still and have a little rest?'

'No fear,' said Tilly's mum firmly. 'You stay where you are.'

Tilly sulked. But by the time they reached the salad cream she'd remembered what she wanted. 'Tuna!' she yelled. 'My favourite sandwich is tuna,' she told Emily. 'With gallons of salad cream. Do you know what? I'm starving.'

She stretched up to a row of cans, just managing to grab one.

But as if Tilly was no one at all – just a little speck of nothing, Tilly thought furiously – Sophie whisked the tin high over Tilly's head.

'No, you don't,' she said. 'Don't you know what happens to dolphins when the fishermen catch the tuna fish . . .?'

And before Tilly had the chance to say no, and she didn't care either, Sophie started to tell the whole supermarket in dreadful detail exactly what did.

Tilly couldn't bear to listen to one more scary thing.

When Tilly didn't want to be scared, the feeling often turned into an angry one. That happened now. Tilly's middle grew hot and tight as if she was going to burst out through her buttons.

'You give that back, Soph,' she said. And her voice sounded hot and tight too. 'Give it back.'

A little boy in dungarees stared at her with frightened eyes.

Sophie was still shouting.

'Give it back, Soph,' Tilly said again, shoving the trolley into her sister's knees with angry little pushes, 'Or I'll do something so bad – you'll fall off your bones.'

The little boy whimpered. His mother picked him up and hurried past as if Tilly was a child in a horror film.

'That's enough, Tilly,' said Tilly's mum, using the tone that usually made Tilly think twice. 'Or you'll wait in the car.'

It was too late. Tilly couldn't behave now if she wanted to.

'GIVE ME BACK MY TUNA!' she roared.

'. . . Then they get tangled up in the nets and however hard they try to swim away they can't, even the babies, and they die and soon there won't be any dolphins left in the sea,' Sophie ranted on.

You'd think Tilly was a monster for being BORN. All she wanted was some tiny little sandwiches for tea.

'SHUT UP! I don't BELIEVE you,' Tilly screamed.

'Oh, shut up both of you,' said their mum crossly. Then to Tilly's surprise, she added, 'Give Tilly her tuna back, Sophie, and stop being such a horrible little know-it-all. If you really want to make the world a better place you could start by being nicer to your own –'

Then something terrible happened.

Right after Tilly's mum said 'know-it-all', Tilly's big sister took a huge gasping breath as if someone had slapped her. Her face crumpled. And right in the middle of the supermarket, Sophie Beany burst into tears.

Tilly wanted to die.

Then, after what felt like years, Sophie said, 'Could you give me the car keys, please.'

Her voice didn't sound like Sophie's voice any more. It sounded like a ghost's. Tilly's mum silently fished the car keys out of her bag. Sophie fled, bumping into people as she ran, as if she couldn't see where she was going properly.

Tilly's mum popped two cans of tuna in her trolley and marched up the aisle humming. Tilly wasn't fooled by that kind of humming. Emily slipped her warm hand into Tilly's chilly one, as if she guessed how bad she felt. Tilly's chin wobbled. She squeezed Emily's hand hard to stop the wobbling getting worse.

Mum scooped up a box of cereal. 'Any more requests?' she said brightly.

'No,' said Tilly. *Her* voice sounded like a ghost's now. She cleared her throat. 'No thank you.'

She was trying not to see those horrible little tins of tuna in the trolley, but they kept shining into the corners of her eyes as if they were proud of causing so much trouble.

At the check-out Mum let Tilly and Emily put the groceries on the conveyor belt while she packed. When she wasn't looking, Tilly slid the tuna out, sneaking the cans behind a sweet display.

All the way home, Sophie stared silently out of the car window. Once, a fat tear rolled down her nose. Sophie didn't seem to know it was there. but Tilly saw it. And Tilly could hear Sophie's weird music leaking out of her earphones through her tangly hair. Sad underwater sounds that made Tilly think of dying baby dolphins.

The moment Tilly's mum parked the car Sophie ran indoors. Emily said probably she'd better not stay to tea, but she squeezed Tilly's hand again so Tilly knew it wasn't her fault.

Tilly's mum marched into the kitchen. 'So I can make the tea in peace and quiet,' she said in a fierce voice. Then she banged the cupboard doors so hard Tilly's rainbow magnet fell off the fridge.

Tom tucked his books under his arm.

'I think I'll do my science homework upstairs,' he said. 'All this peace and quiet is giving me a headache.'

Tilly wandered unhappily into the living-room. Her knees felt wobbly. Her tummy had a hurting kind of emptiness inside it.

'Move, Tilly,' said Kate. 'I can't see the TV.'

Tilly stayed where she was. 'Sophie cried in the supermarket,' she said.

'Why?' asked Kate, astonished. Sophie never cried. Not when anyone could see, anyway.

Tilly threw herself at her big sister and burst into tears. 'She just DID,' she wailed.

That night Tilly couldn't sleep. Usually she loved curling up in her own bed in her own room, trying to decide what to dream about. Dad and Kate had painted the walls sunflower yellow. The curtains were cream, hanging from wooden poles. In the mornings the sun shone through them making friendly patterns. Tilly even had a pinboard and she could put anything she liked on it.

Kate had given her a picture of the earth seen from outer space. It looked blue and very magic. Once, when she had one of her flying dreams, Tilly found herself flying over the Beanys' house in her nightie, up through the sky and up, until the earth sailed below her like a beautiful blue bubble. She wasn't scared because the whole time she was flying she could hear Kate singing in the bath.

Tilly wished she could have that dream again. She'd fly up and find the hole in the sky and mend it somehow, that's what she'd do.

She patted her pillow, wriggling until she found a cool place for her cheek.

Kate's boyfriend, Ollie, had given Tilly a gold

sun to pin on one curtain and three blue butterflies to pin on the other. And there was a rug made out of millions of different coloured ribbons. It was the magickest room ever. She didn't even have to share it with Tom's awful socks like she did at the old house.

But the room didn't feel magic tonight. A lonely-sounding wind blew down the chimney, and muttered in the fireplace.

Probably Sophie couldn't sleep. Probably she thought everyone hated her. Probably she was hungry.

Tilly hadn't been able to eat a thing either. Every time she'd looked across at Sophie's empty chair she'd felt so bad she couldn't swallow even a tiny mouthful.

Without wanting to, Tilly sat up. Then, still not wanting to, she climbed out of bed and padded across the floor, careful not to tread on the creaky parts. She peered through her door. Mum usually left the light on so Tilly could find the bathroom, but the bulb had broken. Tonight the air was full of shadows.

Tilly tiptoed downstairs. When she came back up she was carrying a stripey blue tea-towel wrapped round something that made little clinking sounds. She took a big sobbing breath and fled across the shadowy landing. Then, instead of going back to her own room, she crept up the attic stairs, careful not to catch her feet in the holey carpet. She was so cold her teeth kept bumping together like little pebbles.

A strange sound was coming out of Sophie's door. At first Tilly thought it was crying, then that it was the wind but, suddenly, just as she was going to knock, she thought it might be ghosts and she pulled her hand back in a panic.

'You might as well come in, Tilly,' said Sophie's voice through the door. 'I can hear you breathing like a baby hippo.'

Sophie didn't sound angry, thought Tilly. Only snuffly. She opened the door a crack. 'I can't see,' she said. She was shivering hard now. 'Your dark is rushing out and my eyes feel funny.'

Sophie sighed, rustled and switched her lamp on.

'Thank you,' said Tilly gratefully. She ran, jumped and dived under Sophie's covers .

Sophie yelped. 'Your feet are freezing.'

'All of me is, that's the problem,' said Tilly, trying not to look at Sophie, who had that lopsided look you get when you cry too much.

She unwrapped her tea-towel. Two spoons fell out. Sophie giggled tearily when she saw what else was inside. 'You funny thing. No wonder you're cold.'

'You can eat it, Soph,' said Tilly. 'It hasn't got animal stuff in.'

'Mind if I put the light out again?' asked Sophie, after they'd eaten most of the ice-cream.

'All right,' said Tilly bravely.

It was nice once her eyes were used to it. Sophie's skylight didn't have curtains so Tilly could see a lump of moon floating over the house, and after a while, stars like fierce white sparks. She felt giddy, in an exciting way, as if Sophie's bed was sailing through space like the animals' ark in the story.

'That's spooky music,' said Tilly. 'Is it from *Top of the Pops*?'

Sophie giggled again, hugging her. 'Silly. It's dolphins.'

'Don't fib, Sophie,' said Tilly sternly. 'Dolphins aren't birds, you know.'

'No, really, cross my heart,' said Sophie. 'They sing to their babies like we do.'

'What – lullabies?' Tilly was amazed.

'Well, kind of,' said Sophie.

'I can't understand the words very well,' said Tilly in a worried voice. 'What language is it?'

'Dolphin of course,' said Sophie. 'Dolphins aren't like people. They all speak the same language. Sometimes they don't even talk. They read each other's minds. And they love music. Long ago, if people wanted to call the dolphins they sang to them, and the dolphins came swimming up out of the sea.'

'Like Spike when he hears the fridge door open,' said Tilly amazed.

She wriggled under the covers. The idea that someone could call a dolphin out of the sea by singing was so extraordinary she needed to think about it. 'Are you telling me a story, Soph?' she asked. Usually it was Kate who told Tilly stories.

'Kind of,' said Sophie again, sounding a bit surprised herself. 'But I'm too sleepy to tell you any more,' she added quickly.

Sophie's bed went sailing on through the starry darkness.

It was funny how the moon changed shape. Last time Tilly looked it was all curled up, like a little bitten off fingernail. Tonight it was nearly, but

20

not quite, round; like a wonky soap bubble. And it was looking right back at her, Tilly could tell.

'Does everything sing, do you think, Soph?' she asked after a while. 'Even the moon?'

'Maybe,' said Sophie sleepily.

After a while the tape clicked off. The dolphin singing stopped. Sophie gave a tiny snore.

Tilly patted her sister's shoulder, but gently so as not to wake her.

'Sorry about the dolphins, Soph,' she whispered. 'Sorry about the hole in the sky.'

But the wonky white moon went on staring down at her in Sophie's bed, as if it had something important it wanted to ask her.

'Sorry, moon,' Tilly told the moon drowsily. 'I will try to save the world. Only I don't know how to do it by myself, that's the problem.'

Her eyes began to close.

It might have been a dream. Because Tilly'd never heard anything like it when she was awake. It wasn't sad underwater music like the dolphins made. It was sweet, airy and mysterious. The silvery sound got in her bones as well as her ears, only so gently Tilly felt suddenly peaceful inside. Even with her eyes closed she could feel the moon spreading its light softly across her pillow.

'The moon is singing,' she whispered to herself.

And as though the moon had made a promise to her, and she had made a promise right back to it, Tilly knew everything was going to be all right. I'll tell Sophie tomorrow, she thought, yawning. Everything does sing, even the moon.

She wriggled until she found a comfy bit of Sophie to lean on. And then she went to sleep.

2 The future child

'Aren't you well, Tilly?' Dad asked her next morning. 'You didn't eat your tea and now you haven't had breakfast.'

Tilly looked at her plate, shocked to see her scrambled eggs still there. Mum felt her forehead as she went past, with the hand that wasn't holding the sink plunger.

'Yuck,' said Sophie, who was too close to the plunger. 'Don't put that near me.'

'Nor me,' said Tom. 'I've got my best threads on.' Tom's weird friend Merv said 'threads' when he meant clothes, so now Tom said it too. Tom and Merv were going to a computer exhibition. Tom and Merv loved computers.

'Does thinking give you a temperature?' asked Tilly, puzzled. 'I was only thinking.'

'The drain's blocked again,' said Mum. 'It seems

normal,' she added. 'Tilly's temperature, I mean, not the drain. The drain can't cope with the washing-machine water and the rain at the same time. We need a plumber.'

'Emily's dad's a plumber,' said Tilly, making patterns in the salt. 'He fixes cars too.'

'OK, let's ask Emily's clever dad,' agreed Mum.

Tilly pushed back her chair. 'I'll get him.'

Tilly felt too shy to tell anyone about the moon music this morning, even Sophie. She might tell Emily though.

'Take your coat. It's raining like the end of the world,' said Mum. 'I don't know what's wrong with the weather.'

'It's that old ozone,' said Tilly sighing. 'Miss Hinchin read us a story, I told you. The animals made an ark so they could sail to another planet.'

'Perhaps we should forget the drains and get Emily's dad to build us an ark instead,' Dad said. He sounded a bit jealous. Tilly's dad wasn't much good at drains and things.

'He's not a carpenter, Daddy,' said Tilly, giving him a kiss to cheer him up as she went into the hall. 'Don't you know that?'

Tilly splashed through the yard, up the alley between her house and Emily's and into the street.

Emily's dad was doing something to his van. Rain
dripped off his cap as he fiddled in the engine. He
was singing a lovely tune to himself but the minute
he saw Tilly he looked shy and stopped.

'Morning, Miss Beany,' he said. 'What's

happening?'

'Our drain's blocked,' said Tilly. 'My mum says when you're not busy can you come. Has your van broken?'

'No,' said Emily's dad, sounding shocked. 'This van doesn't have my permission to break yet, you know.'

'Is Emily playing?'

'She wasn't even awake last time I looked. Tell your mum I'll be round later, then come back and cook up some wickedness with Emily, eh?'

'All right,' agreed Tilly, giggling. 'But we're not witches, didn't you know?'

Emily's mum looked tired but she smiled when she saw Tilly on the doorstep. 'Ben kept us up half the night,' she said.

Emily was watching TV. 'Hiya,' she said, yawning.

'Tilly!' yelled Ben happily. Ben wasn't tired at all. He came scooting up on his bottom and hugged Tilly round her knees. Ben was old enough to walk, but something had gone wrong when he was born so his legs didn't work as well as other people's. That's why he had to go to hospital all the time, to see if the doctors could help.

Tilly liked Ben, even if he was a boy. She liked his smiley eyes and the way his hair made little soft

question marks in the
air. And another reason
was that Ben had his
birthday on exactly the
same day as Tilly. He was
her birthday twin!

Ben showed her the
telephone he got for
being good at the hospital
last time. Tilly made the
telephone ring a few
times but at last she
said firmly, 'Not now,
Ben. Emily and I are
busy,' which was what you
had to say if you wanted Ben to leave you alone.

'OK – bye,' Ben said, scooting off.

Tilly plumped down beside Emily. 'Is this
programme good?'

'Don't know,' Emily said sleepily. Sophie always
took ages to wake up too. So Tilly sat quietly
watching pop singers talk about raising money for a
country where there wasn't enough water to grow
food. She looked away when they showed how
hungry the people were.

'Why do we get all the rain?' she said aloud.

'And those people don't get any? Maybe that old hole in the sky is making the weather leak out in the wrong places.'

'Don't know,' Emily yawned again.

Tilly decided it was time Emily woke up. 'I've got a secret, Em,' she said. 'Let's go to our tree.'

Tilly's dad still hadn't mended the wall, so Emily and Tilly just climbed over the bricks to get back into Tilly's garden. Then they raced through the long, wet grass to the wild garden at the bottom. This part didn't really belong to the Beanys. It belonged to an old lady who'd gone to live with her son in Birmingham, leaving her house empty and her garden smothered with weeds and brambles.

Tilly's mum said if someone didn't buy that house soon she was going to plant some potatoes there herself. She hated to see a garden going to waste. But Tilly loved that run-wild garden exactly the way it was, because once you climbed through a sort of archway in another falling-down wall, there was a tree growing that was so old it had hollow insides, like a little room.

To get in, first you had to climb up. Then you jumped down, just a little way. And you were inside an actual tree!

It was Tilly who'd gone exploring and found enough space for her and another Tilly-sized person to squeeze inside without getting stuck. You could even peep through a bumpy window that had grown in the trunk. Tilly was glad about the window. It would be too spooky inside a tree in the dark.

Once they were inside in the dry, Tilly told Emily about the hole in the sky and the whales' lullaby and how everything made its own music. Then she told her about the moon singing to itself in lonely outer space and how Tilly'd promised to help save the world.

'But I can't do it by myself,' Tilly said. 'So you've got to help me.'

Emily was jealous. 'You'd better wake me next time you hear moon music,' she said. 'Throw stones at my window. Mum won't mind. Ben keeps her awake anyway.' That was the good thing about Emily, once she'd woken up. She loved adventures, so long as there weren't any creepy-crawlies in them.

'All right,' Tilly promised. 'But what are we going to do, Em?'

'About the hole in the sky and things?'

Tilly nodded. Emily hunched her shoulders. She

couldn't answer right away because a long beetley thing with whiskers was crawling across one of the walls of the tree room and she was trying not to look.

'Yes,' said Tilly, who understood about Emily and beetles. 'And the weather getting mixed up and everything.'

'Grown-ups don't even know what to do about those things,' said Emily, keeping a careful eye on the beetle.

'Some of them do,' said Tilly. 'Like those pop singers. They're doing that concert.'

'We can't sing,' Emily pointed out. 'Anyway, how can singing mend a hole in the sky? Some things can't be changed, Mum says. We just have to put up with them.' Tilly knew Emily was thinking about Ben.

'He might learn to walk,' said Tilly. 'If he goes to that place they told your mum and dad about.'

Emily shook her head. 'My daddy says it would cost a mint of money,'

'What kind of mint?' asked Tilly at once. 'Minty toothpaste you squeeze out of a tube?'

Emily giggled. 'No, I know! Mint humbugs,' she said. 'The stripey kind. You could suck it and it would last and last and never run out.'

'Peppermint-cream money,' shouted Tilly. 'You could make it in a saucepan.'

'Money with holes like Polos,' shrieked Emily.

A gust of wind blew through the branches.

Emily shivered. 'Did you see where that beetle went?' she asked. She chewed her thumb nervously.

But Tilly was too excited to bothcr about beetles. 'Listen!' she whispered, grabbing Emily's sleeve. She'd banged her elbow but she hardly noticed that either. 'Listen,' she said again. 'Can't you hear it, Em?'

'Hear what?' said Emily. 'I'm freezing. Let's go.' She stretched on tiptoe towards the traily branch you used to pull yourself out of the secrets tree.

'It's stopped,' said Tilly disappointed. 'I heard the moon music again. Like last night. '

'It couldn't be the actual moon, Tilly,' said Emily sensibly. 'It's not night-time.'

'The moon's in the sky all the time,' Tilly explained, scrambling after her. 'Merv told me. It just goes invisible in the daytime or something.'

'Ow,' grumbled Emily. 'I missed it again but I'm too cold to wait out here.'

'Let's go to Beth's house,' said Tilly.

Beth's mum was throwing out some old camping things. Emily, Beth, and Tilly played a noisy game of sliding down the attic stairs inside the old sleeping-bags until Beth's mum asked them to stop before someone got hurt.

So they watched TV while Beth's mum did the ironing. First there was a programme about people who dug up some old treasure in a buried boat

with a dead king in it. Then there was a film about
a girl from the future. You could tell she wasn't
from now because her hair was silver and she wore
her nightdress during the daytime. There was a
pattern on her cheek too, like a tattoo in a comic,
only prettier. The future girl could do amazing
things, except in the future times they weren't that

amazing because even little children could do them.

'If we could meet the future children, they could teach us their magic,' sighed Beth when the film finished, shaking her raggedy fringe out of her eyes.

The room smelled of hot, damp cotton. Beth's mum was ironing the sheets. Her iron kept spurting steam like a little dragon.

'In the old days people would think this television was magic,' said Beth's mum. 'We can do all kinds of things they couldn't. Cure serious illnesses. Travel through the air.'

'Will future people do things we can't, then?' asked Tilly, looking interested.

'Of course,' said Beth's mum. She was trying to fold a sheet in half but her arms weren't long enough. 'Scientists find something new every day,' she said, holding the corners carefully under her chin. 'Discover new stars, invent machines. Sometimes they do it by accident, when they're trying to invent something else.'

'That's true, because do you know,' said Tilly excitedly, 'once I made a Best Friend Machine, but really it was a wishing one and the wishes came true. I'm not lying.'

'I don't know what the future is,' said Beth, looking puzzled. 'Because when does it start, that's what I don't know. I mean, is it tomorrow, or next week or when is it, Tilly?'

'The future's exactly the same as the olden times, only back to front,' Tilly told her.

Beth started shaking her head as if she was trying to get water out of her ears.

'Don't you see?' Tilly explained. 'Some olden times are near to now times, like when I was a baby, and some are a long way away, like history and dinosaurs. And the future's like the past, except the other way round.'

'Oh,' said Beth, in a small voice.

'I didn't understand it at first, either,' said Tilly soothingly.

'All alonc?' said Tilly's dad later, finding Tilly sitting on the window-seat, half-hidden behind the curtains.

'Yes,' said Tilly. 'Because I'm thinking, Daddy, that's why.'

Her dad sat beside her. 'Can I help?'

Tilly frowned. 'I'm thinking how to meet a future girl. Because she could tell us how to put all the bad things right.'

Tilly's dad hugged her. 'Which bad things are those?'

Tilly didn't hug him back. 'Like in the news,' she said. 'You know.'

'Oh, those,' said Dad. 'No wonder you're so serious.'

'Sometimes people dig up stuff from the past,' said Tilly. 'Like boats with dead kings and treasure in them. Daddy, do you know, did they dig up any future treasure yet? Like a bracelet you do time travelling with by twisting it on your arm?'

Tilly's dad shook his head. 'I never heard about it if they did. Why?'

Tilly frowned. 'The future children know things we don't know about yet. How to mend the ozone and everything.' She hugged her knees, rocking herself a tiny bit. 'People don't always have that time bracelet,' she murmured dreamily. 'Sometimes they find an old door no-one else wants.'

Suddenly Tilly Beany sat up very straight.

'Daddy, it might take a long time for a future girl to come here by mistake, mightn't it?'

'I think it might,' agreed Tilly's dad. 'Tilly, your eyes haven't looked so green for a long time. What are you planning?'

'So it would be more sensible, really,' said Tilly smiling now, 'for me to go into the future and find her, wouldn't it?' She patted her dad's arm gently because she knew it might be some time before she saw him again.

'We-ell,' her dad began. 'I don't know if anyone's ever . . . Now where are you off to in such a hurry, Matilda Beany?'

Tilly had jumped down off the window-seat, her eyes shining. 'Only to Nessa's and everyone's,' she told him. 'Don't worry. I'll be very careful if we do find the door into the future. And when we come back we'll be so wise we'll know how to make everything turn out all right, OK?'

Tilly was so excited she felt a bit sick. First she had to find Nessa, though, because Nessa had the best face paints. If Tilly and her friends were going into the future, it would be better if they looked as if they belonged there. The nighties were easy. The silver hair was more of a problem. In the end Beth's mum lent them some silver Christmas tree ribbons, the very thin spaghetti kind, and helped tie them beautifully in their hair.

Getting ready to visit the future was taking longer than Tilly had planned. It was almost teatime when the four girls in their nighties (except for Nessa who had pyjamas, but Tilly said that didn't matter), with their specially painted faces and silvery hair ribbons climbed over the broken wall into Tilly's garden.

The sun was shining, that was one good thing.

But Beth's tummy was rumbling. 'What if I don't like the dinners they have there?' she said, worried. 'What if it's purple?'

'Or really slimy,' agreed Nessa. 'And they make you eat it.'

Tilly sighed. 'We are trying to save the world, you know,' she said.

'I'm going to ask my mum for biscuits,' said sensible Emily. 'Because anyway, Tilly, what if future people don't need to eat food?'

Tilly hadn't thought of that. 'You'd better then,' she agreed.

'So what are we looking for again?' asked Beth later, after everyone had eaten two biscuits to be on the safe side.

'A door,' said Tilly. 'Or a time bracelet. A door would be better because only one person could use the bracelet and you'd all have to hold on to me.'

'And someone might let go,' agreed Beth shivering. 'And fall into the wrong bit of future, and stay there all by themselves for ever.'

'I was wondering, Tilly, will they have beetles in the future?' asked Emily.

'They didn't say about them in the programme,' said Tilly. 'That's all I know.'

'Is the future door in this garden, then?' asked Nessa.

'Yes,' Tilly said firmly. 'We've already walked past it millions of times without seeing it.'

'Didn't you see it either, Tilly?' Nessa asked.

'You never do see it, till it's the right time,' Tilly explained.

'I keep forgetting that,' said Nessa.

Beth was getting goose-pimples. 'I hope it's warm in the future,' she shivered.

'It's warm as hot toast,' Tilly promised. 'It isn't always an actual door you go through, you know,' she added. 'Sometimes it's an old archway that looks really ordinary and . . .' Tilly's expression changed. 'Oh – oh, everyone! You've got to follow me,' she shouted. 'I know where it is!'

She began racing towards the wild end of the garden. 'Follow me,' she yelled again. 'And do you know why? Because listen – I can hear the moon music and it's really loud.'

This time everyone heard the mysterious silvery sound.

Emily, Beth and Nessa started to run after her.

'Ooh, Tilly, the music makes me feel peaceful inside, just like you said,' said Emily breathlessly.

'I know,' Tilly shouted. 'But hurry, because if the moon music stops we mightn't be able to get through the door, that's what I think.'

They followed each other bravely through the gap in the falling-down wall without looking back even once.

'You see,' said Tilly opening her arms wide. 'You can feel it's the future now, can't you?'

'Yes,' agreed Nessa. 'The sun is so much brighter.'

'I'm still a bit cold,' said Beth doubtfully.

But Tilly was running again, past the secrets tree, which looked almost exactly the same as it did in Tilly's own time, into the tunnel of an overgrown shrubbery and out again.

And there, under the old apple trees, in the bright sunlight of the future, was a baby in a wooden cradle, drowsily playing with its own fingers.

Emily was so excited she didn't notice Tilly had stopped in front of her and they bumped heads.

'Emmy, Emmy! A future baby!' whispered Tilly.

'Ohhh,' breathed Emily amazed. 'Is that her mother, then?'

Sitting on an old chair under a rambling rose that was dropping red petals everywhere, was a girl not much older than Kate. She didn't look like a nowadays mother. She was wearing a long floaty skirt, three or four kinds of silvery earrings in each ear and her top was so short you could see almost all her tummy. She was singing something that sounded like a future lullaby and sewing something lacey. The girl's hair wasn't silver, only brown, but she had brightly coloured threads plaited into a long strand of it, so Tilly just knew she was from the future. She was so excited she started to laugh.

The girl looked up. 'Hello,' she said, startled. 'Which planet do you little ones come from?'

Tilly laughed. 'We're not aliens, don't worry. Actually we've come from the olden times,' she explained, pushing her silver ribbons out of her eyes. 'I'm Tilly.'

'We need some future people to help us,' Beth said. She was having trouble with her ribbons too.

'We've got to save the world,' Emily said shyly. 'Tilly heard the moon singing and she promised.'

'Only we don't know how, that's the problem,' said Tilly. 'That's why we had to find the door into your times.'

Nessa was stroking the baby's tiny hand. 'What's her name?' she asked.

'Maya Rose,' said the girl. 'Because she was born in the month of May and she looked so exactly like a little rose.'

Tilly's eyes grew enormous. 'Ohhh,' she said. That's just what a future person would say. It was like poetry. 'Is Maya very wise do you know?' she asked softly.

The girl smiled. 'Well, she looks wise to me,' she said. 'But all babies do, don't they? It's hard to be sure until she can talk.' She was going to say something else, but loud rock music started playing inside the house, making everyone jump. 'I told him to turn that thing down,' said Maya's mum crossly.

'Kate's boyfriend Ollie likes that song,' said Tilly surprised. 'It's new in our times. Do you have it in the future then?'

But just then the wind blew in a fierce little gust and Tilly heard the moon music again, puzzlingly close this time. At the same moment she looked up into the tree and saw the wind chimes hanging among the tiny green apples like silver flutes. Every time the wind blew, the chimes knocked softly against each other, making a clear sweet sound.

It was wind music Tilly heard in the night, not moon music at all.

She stamped her foot and her eyes filled with tears. 'This isn't the future after all is it?' she said. 'So how can we find the real door anyway? That's what I don't know.' And she began to cry because she could hear the disc jockey's stupid voice on the radio and she just hated these now times, where horrible things were happening everywhere and not even grown-ups knew how to stop them.

'Don't cry sweetheart,' said the girl. 'I don't think you've made a mistake. I think you've come to the right place. Maybe I can't help you but one day Maya will be a future person. So will you, Tilly. And you and Maya might be some of the people who help to save the world.'

'And I will, won't I?' said Nessa, feeling left out.

'Look,' said the girl, 'I've got to feed Maya now. Come back another day, if your mums say you can, and have some tea. My name's Naomi.'

'Thank you,' said Tilly, wiping her eyes on her sleeve.

'It won't be a purple tea will it?' said Beth, who was still a bit puzzled about what was happening.

'No,' promised Naomi laughing. 'I'm trying to give up the purple sort.'

'So we did find a kind of future door,' Tilly told Kate while Kate helped her untie the silver ribbons. 'And those were very special wind chimes anyway, not the usual kind. They were moon chimes, I think. And guess what? We found a future baby, and do you know, she's called Maya Rose and when she grows up she's going to be very wise and help us save the world.'

'Till then, how about a hot bath?' said Kate rubbing Tilly's chilly hands. 'And maybe we should wash this beautiful pattern off your face. Unless you're planning to visit the future tomorrow?'

'No,' laughed Tilly. 'I'm staying in these times now until they turn into the future times.'

'Good idea,' said Kate. 'That way you can make

sure Maya Rose grows up as wise as wise can be.'

Tilly was so astonished she stopped halfway up the stairs in her vest and knickers. 'That's what I was going to do, Kate. How did you know?'

'Sister magic,' said Kate, smiling. 'That's how.'

3 Wild things

When Tilly and her mum walked to school on Monday they saw Naomi at the bus stop. Naomi was carrying Maya on her back in a kind of home-made rucksack. Naomi waved and Tilly and her mum waved back.

'I'm glad someone's living in that house at last, even if it doesn't strictly belong to them,' said Tilly's mum.

'Did they steal it, then?' asked Tilly, her eyes enormous.

'Not exactly steal,' said Mum. 'More like borrow. Houses need to be loved, the way cats need to be stroked, otherwise they get lonely and fade away. Houses shouldn't be left empty when there are people with nowhere to live. I wonder if they'll do the garden,' she added thoughtfully.

Tilly knew her mum loved gardens, so she didn't say that sometimes wild things need places just to go wild in, without people always telling them to climb poles or march in straight rows or stop dropping their petals on the grass. That's what Tilly thought anyway. But aloud she said, 'I think Maya's mummy likes it just wild.'

Mum laughed. 'You mean you do. You're an outlaw, Tilly. Like Robin Hood.'

'Emily's one too,' said Tilly. 'Except for she hates creepy-crawlies. Do you know, can outlaws go home when it's dark?'

'Maybe if you're an outlaw you start enjoying the dark after a while,' suggested Mum.

Tilly pulled a face. 'Probably I'm a daytime outlaw then,' she said. Tilly couldn't imagine anyone enjoying the dark, except maybe witches.

As Tilly dashed past the staffroom, Miss Hinchin caught her.

'Tilly, could you look after our visitor? I've got to make a phone call.'

Miss Hinchin's cheeks were pink, as if she felt too warm. And she was much much smilier than normal. The visitor had a pile of picture books under one arm, and in his other hand he carried an art folder just like Ollie Pyke's. He was wearing boots like Ollie's too, only newer. He had that floppy film star hair which gets in your eyes, and he looked a bit nervous.

Of course! This was the writer who'd written that horrible story, Tilly remembered.

'My classroom's down here,' she told him in her sternest voice, starting to march down the corridor.

'I'm Mike Ryan,' said the writer, trying to keep up.

'I know,' said Tilly, over her shoulder. 'Miss Hinchin read us your scary old book.'

'Aren't you going to tell me your name now?' asked Mr Ryan, dropping one of his books.

'It's Tilly Beany,' said Tilly Beany, marching fiercely past Miss Angel's room. Miss Angel's babies were there already, sitting on the carpet, holding their two thumbs straight up in the air like little TV aeriels, listening to Miss Angel. Miss Angel taught the youngest infants and she wore swingy short skirts and long boots. She wore her plaits in a kind of fountain so that every bit of her danced when

she moved. Miss Angel's babies just loved her.

'They look terribly well-behaved,' said the writer.

'Miss Angel has a magic trick, that's why,' said Tilly, 'so they have to be good. Are all your stories like that sky one?' she added. 'Or are some of them quite nice?'

'I hope some of them are quite nice,' said Mike Ryan. 'I try to make them nice.' He looked worried.

'What didn't you like?'

'I didn't like how it made me cry and cry,' said Tilly, 'I was scared Spike would fly away. Then Sophie and me had a huge fight in the supermarket. Mum shouted. Then Sophie cried. It was about the tuna fish anyway.'

'That's awful,' said Mike. 'I don't want to make children cry. I just want people to think about the damage we're doing to the planet.'

He looked as if he wanted to cry now.

'It isn't the children doing the damage, didn't you know that?' Tilly explained. 'It's the grown-ups you should frighten. Anyway,' she added in a kinder voice, 'don't worry. Sophie and me made friends. I brought her some ice-cream in the night. Then I slept in her bed and I heard the moon music. Do you know what, instead of scary books you should write one to say how the children save the world, that's what you should do.'

Miss Hinchin had caught them up now. 'Tilly,' she said, sounding shocked. 'Don't be so rude.'

'She was only being honest,' said Mike. 'She's given me some things to think about.'

'Oh – really?' said Miss Hinchin, tossing her hair a bit as if she didn't quite believe him. She was still pink, Tilly noticed, and smelled unusually flowery, as if she'd sprayed on extra perfume while she was on the phone.

'Tilly's great company,' said the writer firmly.

Tilly gave him a warm smile. She thought she might enjoy having a visiting writer after all.

Later, Mike Ryan sat on Miss Hinchin's table, running his hands through his floppy hair, telling them how he'd been crazy about animals since he was small. He showed them pictures of pets he'd had and tiny books he'd written about them when he was only the same age as Tilly. One of the pets was only a worm he'd found in the garden. Another one was a secret guinea pig he'd kept in a shoe box under his bed, 'Until my mum heard it whistling,' said the writer grinning. Tilly grinned too, and when Miss Hinchin passed the scruffy little books round, Tilly gave her a specially hard stare, because Mr Ryan's handwriting was worse than Tilly's had ever been. And he was an actual writer now, so there!

Tilly decided she was going to make a book about Spike. In her book Spike was going to wear a suit with an S on it, like Superman and he'd stop the animals flying away just before they reached the moon. 'Just give the humans one more chance,' he'd say. 'They'll change, I'll take care of that.'

She was so busy planning her own story she forgot to listen to Mr Ryan. When she remembered again, the writer was saying that he liked visiting schools to talk about taking care of the planet. He showed them a picture of a saint called St Francis who used to talk to birds.

'So caring about the planet isn't a new thing,' Mike said. 'Some people have always loved the wild things of the earth.'

Tilly wished she could talk to the birds like that saint. No, she wished they would talk to her. The first thing she'd ask them is how do you actually fly? Because that's something Tilly really needed to know. Sometimes she thought she could remember, and then she'd realise it was just in a flying dream she'd done it, and not real at all.

Then Mike Ryan said something that made Tilly jump out of her skin. He told them that in some parts of the world there used to be special wild places where only wild things were allowed to live. Humans mustn't visit them, or even peep at them, that's how wild the places were.

'Some Africans and Native Americans believe trees and plants have spirits living in them,' Mr Ryan said. 'But spirits are shy creatures. They hate crowds and factories, noise and car fumes. So they only come out, just before dawn, or at twilight when the world is very still.'

Tilly couldn't believe it! The writer was saying exactly the same things Tilly was thinking on the way to school. That was so amazing it made her feel shivery all up her back. Mr Ryan didn't say what the spirits did when they came out, so Tilly supposed they probably just danced around a bit, like when Tilly had to do the wheat dance, and ate a few berries and things and played with the other spirits before they went back to their plants.

Then Mr Ryan told them one special name for tree spirits, which was 'dryad'. Dryad was a Greek word. Ancient Greeks believed in plant spirits too, Mike said. And he drew a scribbly picture of one on his big art pad, looking out of a kind of window in a tree trunk.

And then, to Tilly's astonishment, out of the scribblings came a girl just like Tilly, except her hair had a lovely crown of leaves in it. Tilly Beany's eyes grew enormous. Mr Ryan gave her a secret wink.

'Ooer, that's you, Tilly,' said Shazna, giggling.

'Does that peculiar girl live in that uncomfortable looking tree then?' Bernice asked, her toffee brown eyes narrowing like a cat's. 'Instead of in a proper house like normal people?'

'In a way,' said Mike. 'But she doesn't just live in it. In a way she belongs to it and the tree belongs to her. If someone cuts her tree down she'll die.'

'That's stupid,' said Steven, going red. Steven always went red when he was upset. 'That doesn't make sense.'

But Tilly was still staring at the tree Tilly.

'Do you see why it's so important to keep planting new trees and to keep looking after the trees we still have?' Mr Ryan asked them. 'Now I've never seen a real dryad, and maybe they only happen in stories. And I honestly don't know if there are any tree spirits left anywhere in the world, but I do know that if we keep chopping forests down to make doors and fences and toilet seats and . . .'

'. . . Crayons,' said the Quiet Twin suddenly, making everyone jump. 'Crayons are wooden aren't they?'

'Yes, right – and crayons,' said Mike Ryan

quickly, but you could tell the surprise had made him forget what he meant to say next. 'Because – er, if one day we wake up to find there are almost no wild things left, it won't just be the wild creatures that suffer,' he went on. 'Everyone in this room, all your mums, dads, little brothers and sisters, everyone on this planet will suffer too. The wild things need us and we need the wild things you see, if we want the Earth, our home, to be happy and healthy.'

'Are you feeling all right, Tilly?' whispered Miss Hinchin.

Tilly nodded. It was just a shock to come face to face with a wild Tilly without any warning, and to hear a stranger speaking her own wild early morning thoughts aloud for everyone to hear.

'Now,' said Mr Ryan. 'Everyone tell me the names of some animals that have become extinct.'

Nathan giggled. 'Why does he want to know about animals that stink?' he asked Steven.

Miss Hinchin took a deep breath and explained that 'extinct' meant there wasn't even one kind of that animal left anywhere on the planet.

'Call out some names, everyone. Don't be shy. Then I'll draw them on the board and we'll put them in the story we're going to write together,' said Mr Ryan, getting some chalks out of his art case. He was enjoying himself now.

'Dinosaurs,' yelled Joe at once.

'Good, dinosaurs,' agreed Mike, starting to draw.

'I was going to say them,' said Adam sadly. 'That's all the ones I know.'

'And dodos, silly,' said Alice. 'They couldn't fly, that's how they got extinct.'

Mike Ryan drew a tubby dodo bird next, with feeble little wings like feather dusters.

'Dodo-brain,' Steven whispered to Adam.

Anil waved his arm. 'Sabre-toothed tigers!' he shouted.

'Oh no, not them as well,' said Adam. 'I didn't know they were extinct too. So what's left then?'

'I think pandas are only almost extinct,' said Pritesh. 'I think there's two or four or something in a zoo.'

'I know! A hairy smelly monster,' yelled Nathan, 'with horrible red eyes in the palms of its hands.'

'I don't think hairy monsters are extinct actually, Nathan,' said Adam sounding worried.

'Did you ever see one?' giggled Nathan. 'No? Well then.'

'But being extinct isn't the same as . . .' Poor

Adam couldn't explain what he meant.

'Couldn't we fit a sweet little unicorn somewhere in this story?' asked Bernice, her head on one side, so her silky brown hair went whisk, whisk like a shiny little curtain.

'You see, Nathan, there just never were any hairy monsters,' said Adam desperately. 'So how could they become extinct?'

Tilly stopped listening and began making up a story in her head about a beautiful island where the extinct animals were all living safely and happily. As more and more animals got extinct the island got fuller and fuller. Luckily it was the stretchy kind of island so no one fell off. The thing was, the animals were just teasing, playing a specially long game of hide-and-seek until the humans missed them enough to come and find them. Then they would come charging from behind the trees like the Wild Things doing the Wild Rumpus in that picture book Tilly had, yelling, 'Ha ha, scared you, that time! Well, say sorry then and we'll all come home.'

Tilly was going to write that story and do all her own illustrations, like Mike Ryan.

But after break something happened that was nearly as amazing as Tilly's story.

'Mr Ryan and I have been talking, children,' Miss Hinchin said. 'And we told the headmistress about the work you're doing on the environment.' She paused and Tilly got ready to cover her ears.

'Don't, don't, don't talk about the little baby seals, Miss Hinchin,' she whispered. And to her relief Miss Hinchin didn't.

'And Mrs Grosgrain,' Miss Hinchin went on, looking pink again, 'has promised to let the school have a piece of the school field to turn into a wild area of our own.'

'Wow, a wild area,' said Stephanie, beaming all over her face. 'So what does that mean?' she whispered to Tilly.

'It's not much to look at yet,' Miss Hinchin told them, 'but we're going to make a pond for fish and frogs and we'll plant trees and special plants to attract birds and butterflies. '

'And you're all going to help, kids, aren't you?' asked Mr Ryan, pushing back his floppy hair.

'Ye-s,' yelled everyone.

'So I want you to go home and ask your mums, dads, brothers and sisters to help us, because before the end of term we're going to have a special Wild Day here to raise money,' said Miss Hinchin.

'And we're going to make this the Wildest

School in the World aren't we?' said Mr Ryan.

'Ye-s!' everyone yelled again.

'But what does that mean?' Stephanie whispered again.

Miss Hinchin didn't look too sure either, but she went on, 'So now we're all going to think of some things we can do for our Wild Day, because after lunch Mr Ryan will be visiting Miss Angel's babies.'

'Ow,' moaned everyone jealously.

Tilly had loads of ideas for Wild Day, but Miss Hinchin didn't always like Tilly's kind of idea, so she sat on her hands to stop them waving in the air. But she couldn't believe it. No one said anything. Miss Hinchin peeled a tiny bit of varnish off her thumb nail and Mike Ryan fiddled with the lace in one of his boots. Tilly thought the silence was going to go on for ever. Then there was a soft little rustling sound, like something unfolding tiny new wings, and someone whispered, 'Miss – could we have a Monster Show? Like Miss World, you know, Miss.

With sparkly crowns for prizes.'

It was Leena, the Silent Twin!

No one but Beena had heard Leena say one word in school before. No one had even heard Leena sneeze! The astonished children laughed and clapped. Everyone wanted to see the monsters waddling around in sparkly Miss World crowns.

'But not bikinis,' added Beena, the Quiet Twin, quickly in her soft little voice. 'Because the monsters would be the wrong shape.'

'Mmn,' agreed the Silent Twin nodding . 'A bit too bulgy.'

Tilly laughed so much she got stomach ache. Everyone was laughing. Miss Hinchin kept saying 'Sssh!' but she was laughing too, and Mike Ryan had real tears in his eyes.

When the room was nearly quiet again, Tilly put up her hand.

'We could have a café that was an animals' ark,' she said. 'And decorate it with dodos and tigers and everything.'

'I can give you some animal paintings if you like,' said Mike Ryan. 'I can even help you make an ark.'

'Nothing scary though,' said Tilly sternly.

'Absolutely not,' promised Mike.

'We could build the ark out of old junk like in your story,' said Adam.

'And the mums and dads can bring refreshments for the café and the children can dress up as Wild Things for waiters, and the food can have special environment names,' said Tilly, running out of breath.

'Like Ozone Layer Cake,' suggested Miss Hinchin giggling. 'I'll make that.'

'And Rain Forest Punch,' said Joe. 'With fruit and leaves in it. My dad makes brilliant punch.'

'We could plant trees,' said Shazna. 'My brother works at a plant nursery.'

'The little brothers and sisters can help,' said Anil. 'And when they start at this school they can come and look for their special tree they planted.'

'If we do make a wild area, will the Wild Things stay after all?' asked the Silent Twin in her feathery little whisper. 'I want them to stay, I do.'

The Quiet Twin grabbed a lock of her sister's hair and began twisting it tightly round her fingers. 'And I do,' she said.

'I do too,' said Steven gruffly, his face still red.

Everyone was jumping out of their seats, shouting out ideas, forgetting about putting up their hands. And the really astonishing thing was,

Miss Hinchin didn't even notice!

Just before afternoon home time, Tilly had to run down to the far end of the school to take a message to Mrs Grosgrain. But as she went past Miss Angel's room she heard a terrible din. She peeped in.

Miss Angel's babies were running all over the room like escaped fieldmice. They were climbing on desks, knocking books off the shelves, squeaking, squabbling and poking their fingers in each other's eyes. It was worse than the Wild Rumpus.

Waving his arms in the middle of the classroom was poor Mr Ryan. Tilly could see he was shouting but she couldn't hear him through the noise.

'Oh dear,' said Tilly. 'Someone should help him.'

She opened the door and went in.

'Oh, Tilly,' said Mr Ryan gratefully. 'I made them pretend to be wild animals and they can't seem to stop.'

'Where's Miss Angel?' Tilly yelled in his ear.

'She slipped out for a minute,' said Mr Ryan hoarsely. 'What should I do?'

'Don't worry,' said Tilly. 'Just copy me.' And she sat down in Miss Angel's chair holding up her thumbs like little TV aeriels.

Miss Angel's babies didn't seem to slow down at all and they still carried on roaring round the room

being tigers and gorillas, but you could see that now they were watching Tilly warily out of the corners of their eyes like tiny wild ponies.

'All right, class,' Tilly said, copying Miss Angel's slow clear speaking voice. 'Now, "tune in", everyone.'

'"Tune in", everyone,' Mr Ryan echoed, obediently holding up his thumbs. 'But what good will that do?' he whispered. 'What we need, Tilly, is a large fire extinguisher.'

'It's all right,' Tilly whispered back. 'Miss Angel's magic always works. Look!'

And one by one Miss Angel's babies sat down cross-legged on the carpet without so much as another squeak, holding their thumbs in the air, good as gold.

'How did you do that?' said Mr Ryan, astonished.

'I told you, it's Miss Angel's magic,' said Tilly. 'They'll stay stuck like that now, until you tell them to do something else.'

'Let's leave them like this until Miss Angel comes back' said Mike, closing his eyes. 'It's been a long long day.'

Tilly took her friends, Emily, Nessa and Beth to the Wild Day. They bought balloons with SAVE OUR

66

WILD THINGS written on them and let them float high into the air and out of sight. Tilly's sister Kate and her boyfriend Ollie did a puppet show about Hansel and Gretel, only, in this story, Hansel and Gretel made friends with the wild animals and

together they got rid of the wicked witch who'd been cutting down trees and spoiling the forest for everyone.

Sophie and her friend Rose did the face-painting stall. Tilly's mum and dad helped run the Animals' Ark Café and Tilly bought some of Miss Hinchin's Ozone Layer Cake with her pocket money. Miss Hinchin was running around in a jumper and jeans and dangly earrings selling raffle tickets. Jeans! Tilly couldn't believe it.

Mike Ryan helped judge the Monster Contest. Everyone laughed as the monsters lolloped round the stage to the Miss World music. One shiny green sea monster with fishes and seaweed hanging out of its pockets, was even doing disco dancing!

Third prize went to one of Miss Angel's babies in a gorilla suit. Joint second prize went to Steven and Nathan squeezed into one big pantomime monster costume.

But when the sea monster came dancing up the steps to receive first prize, and took off her shiny green monster head to bow, everyone gasped. Smiling shyly at the audience, with her dark hair tumbling down her shoulders was Leena, the Silent Twin.

Then Tom, Merv and some of their friends played an old pop song called 'Wild Thing', and Anil's little sister helped someone important in a beautiful suit cut the green ribbon that led to the Wild Area.

As the Beanys were leaving they saw Mike Ryan and Miss Hinchin trying to get through the school gate at the same time as a big bunch of balloons.

'This Huge Day is a wild success isn't it,' Miss Hinchin giggled.

'I wanted to give you this,' said Mr Ryan holding out his drawing of the tree Tilly, properly painted now, and framed like a real picture. 'This is to say sorry for my scary book,' he said. 'I'll do better next time.'

'Thank you,' said Tilly shyly.

Then Mr Ryan started to laugh. 'Tell you what, if the planet does start to run out of wild things, all we need to do is borrow Miss Angel's babies. They're the wildest things I've ever seen.' He winked at Tilly and held up his thumbs. '"Tune in",

Tilly Beany,' he said.

'"Tune in", Mr Ryan,' said Tilly, winking back.

And Mike Ryan and Miss Hinchin went giggling out through the school gate with Miss Hinchin's balloons bobbing above their heads like friendly baby planets.

But just before they were out of sight, Tilly noticed something so amazing she had to poke Emily and make her look too.

Miss Hinchin and Mr Ryan were holding hands.

4 The dolphin song

'I can smell the sea,' said Tilly. Warm salt wind whipped her hair across her mouth. 'I promise I don't mind if I don't meet a mermaid,' she told her sister Kate.

'Where did we put the matches?' asked Mum suddenly.

'In the biscuit tin,' said Tilly's dad. 'So they won't get damp.'

'So what did you do with the biscuits?' asked Mum.

'I want to see a dolphin instead,' Tilly went on. 'If you sing they come right up out of the water. Sophie said, didn't you, Soph?'

The Beany family were going to the sea. They couldn't stay with Aunt Rose this time, so Tilly's parents had borrowed some camping things. It was such a squash in the car, there wasn't even room

71

for Tilly to breathe.

'I've never been camping, have I?' said Tilly for the tenth time.

'You'll love it,' said Kate again. 'The important thing is we can walk down to the sea in just a few minutes.'

'The other important thing Kate isn't mentioning,' said Sophie, 'is that if you want the bathroom in the night you'll need a torch. It's so dark in the country you won't be able to see a thing. '

'Oh,' said Tilly, making up her mind she would never need the bathroom at night *ever*, until she was safely back home.

'Anyway this is the wrong kind of sea for dolphins, dumbo,' said Tom grinning.

'Oh,' said Tilly again. Then she said fiercely, 'You don't know everything, Tom Beany. There could be one little lost dolphin, so there.'

'Well, sorree,' said Tom.

'Keep your hair on everyone,' said Dad. 'Almost there.'

He turned up a tiny narrow lane so overhung with trees it was like driving under a green roof.

'Yuck, Tom, you've got spooky green leaves all over you,' giggled Tilly.

But then the car came out of the spooky green tunnel into a sunny field where several tents already billowed gently in the breeze.

'This is it, folks,' said Dad.

'You never said there'd be other people here,' grumbled Sophie.

The Beanys climbed out. Mum passed round the big bottle of lemonade.

'So where shall we pitch our tent?' asked Dad.

'Somewhere we don't have to look at the other campers,' said Sophie at once.

'Not on an ant-hill,' said Tom, wiping his mouth.

'Or where the wind can blow the cooking stove out,' said Tilly's mum, giving the bottle back to Tilly. Tilly was so thirsty she wanted to keep drinking for ever.

'So we can have a lovely view when we're eating breakfast,' said Kate.

'Aaaargh,' cried Dad, putting his hands over his ears.

Dad and Tom started arguing about fitting the tent poles together. Tilly wandered off. She couldn't see how those bits of old bent climbing frame and canvas could ever make a tent. She wanted to be back in the Beanys' own friendly house in her friendly bed with Spike curled up behind her knees like a warm little cushion.

Where was the bathroom anyway? There was an old wagon and a bucket with a hole in it and there was a water tap sticking out of some metal piping. There were even some chickens on the other side of a low fence, complaining to an invisible someone in tiny muffled voices. But Tilly couldn't see a bathroom anywhere.

Kate was feeding grass over a gate to a very tall horse. 'His nose feels *so* soft, like new ballet shoes,' said Kate. 'Feel, Tilly.'

'His teeth are too yellow,' shuddered Tilly. 'He should clean them. Kate, where's the loo?'

Kate pointed to the rickety shed beside the chicken pen.

Tilly's eyes widened. She couldn't. She just couldn't! 'Ask Mum if I can stay with Aunt Rose till it's time to go home,' she pleaded. 'Ple-ease, Kate.'

'Aunt Rose has got those ladies staying,' Kate reminded her. 'Come on, Tilly, it won't be so bad. I'll show you.'

Kate was right. Once you opened the toilet door it was perfectly nice inside.

'But why does it smell like hot tar?' asked Tilly, wrinkling her nose.

'Creosote,' Kate corrected.

'What if the chickens spy on you through the cracks?' said Tilly. 'That's the problem.'

Tilly didn't trust chickens because of how they stared at you creepily out of the corners of their beady little eyes. She didn't like the floppy bits of swimming hat on their heads either; but most of all she hated their feet that looked like giants' dirty old toenails.

'Help me blow up the airbeds, Tilly,' said Kate. 'I'll put mine next to yours.'

'Thank you, Kate,' said Tilly gratefully. 'Because

I haven't been camping before, have I?'

But by the time Kate and Dad had cooked supper on the borrowed barbecue, Tilly knew she loved camping. Tilly's best thing was the pudding; baked bananas with chocolate tucked inside.

After supper Tilly and Tom fetched the water for washing-up.

'Like Little House on the Prairie,' said Tilly enchanted. After that everyone went for a walk. Except Sophie, who was zipped up inside her sleeping-bag listening to her headphones.

In the lane, Tilly found hundreds of pale flowers floating like lilies in the evening air. They smelled exactly like macaroons. But when she tried to pick one for her mum, all the other flowers came too, like a pink necklace on a long twisty string. They were called 'granny's nightcaps', Mum told her. From when grannies wore frilly caps and shawls. Tilly only had one granny and you had to call her Susan. She wore bright-coloured suits from Marks and Spencer and silly high heels with proper tights you had to be careful of the whole time.

'Quick, Tilly, can you see the baby rabbits?' said Dad.

At first Tilly couldn't, because they were exactly the same colour as the earth and they were crouching down as still as little stones. Then one sprang high into the air, making Tilly jump, and after that she spotted five more playing a game of chase. Tom only saw three.

When they got back to the tent, Mum made hot chocolate. 'It gets cold so you need something warm before you go to sleep,' she told Tilly.

The gas lantern was making a sleepy hissing sound. Suddenly the tent looked much friendlier.

Kate started singing, 'You'll never get to heaven.' Tilly and Mum joined in. So did Tom and Dad.

'Oh, you'll never get to heaven on roller-skates,
'Cos you'll roll right past those pearly gates.'

Then everyone, even Sophie, sang a round that Kate had learned at school. The problem with rounds was Tilly was never exactly sure when it was her turn.

Next Tilly had to brush her teeth. She stood at the tap swooshing toothpaste round her mouth. The last birds went zipping over her head. The dry grass tickled her bare feet. Under her breath she sang, 'Oh, you'll never get to heaven, in a sardine tin.'

Then Mum said, 'One last trip to the loo, Matilda Beany,' and Kate and Tilly went racing over the field. Tilly took the torch, even though there was some pink sunset left in the sky.

The tar smell was stronger in the dark and the hens were still grumbling to someone invisible but somehow, after all that singing, Tilly didn't mind the rickety outside loo. 'I'm a night-time outlaw now, aren't I, Kate? ' she said.

All the way back to the tent she waved the

torch, making wildly dancing circles of light. 'Did you see us coming, Dad?' she shouted. 'Did you?'

Then Kate zipped her into her sleeping-bag and Tilly fell asleep. Just like that.

Then all at once she was wide awake in the dark again, all by herself, listening to everyone's breathing sounds. And though for a long time she tried to pretend she didn't, Tilly needed the bathroom very badly again. It was a lonely feeling.

'Kate,' Tilly whispered at last.

'What?'

'I need the loo. '

'Oh, Tilly,' Kate groaned. 'Are you sure?'

'Very, very sure,' said Tilly. 'Sorry.'

It took sleepy Kate ages to unfasten the tent. It made a noise like someone unzipping an enormous pair of jeans really slowly.

Tilly started to giggle but then they were out in the moonlit field all by themselves and it was so amazing she forgot how to breathe.

'Look at the sky, Tilly,' whispered Kate, wide awake now.

Tilly had never seen such dark darkness or such very bright brightness in her life. All in one ordinary little field.

Shivering now, she slid her hand into her big

sister's. 'It's . . .' she started to say. 'It's very . . .' But Tilly couldn't think of a word to describe how it felt to be standing in the country darkness, looking up at trillions of stars so bright they hurt her eyes.

At last she whispered, 'It's not very friendly is it, Kate? But it's very . . . alive.'

Even when she was back inside her sleeping-bag and her shivers had stopped, she couldn't stop thinking how strange it was to go to sleep with just a thin bit of tent between her and all that fiercely blazing light.

'Kate?' Tilly whispered.

'Mmmn?'

'I can feel the stars tingling in the ends of my hair.'

'Mmmn,' said Kate turning over.

'It's very hard to go to sleep, actually,' Tilly whispered to herself, 'with so much tingling.' And then she whispered, wriggling deeper into her sleeping-bag. 'I might find a dolphin tomorrow. So there, Tom Beany.'

Next day when the Beanys went to the beach, Kate and Sophie were so tired they were no fun at all. They just rubbed sun-cream on each other, stretched silently out on their towels and shut their eyes. Tilly's mum rubbed cream on Tilly too and made her wear a baggy T-shirt even though it was warm.

'When I was little, no one worried about the sun,' said Mum. 'But now you have to be careful.'

'Are you going to sunbathe, Tom?' asked Tilly sadly.

'Nah, sunbathing's boring,' said Tom.

'Yippee! Play on the rocks with me then,' said Tilly. Tom was loads nicer on holiday, she thought, without boring old Merv to spoil things.

But Tilly didn't play on the rocks for long because Tom found her a sweet little flower, only, when he poked a piece of seaweed near it the flower opened its petals wide then closed tightly around it, like a greedy little mouth.

'Is that a fish pretending to be a flower?' said Tilly alarmed.

'It's only a sea anemone, silly,' Tom told her.

Tilly didn't like things that pretended to be other things. It gave her a dizzy, unsafe feeling. Like the time she found Spike sleeping in the compost heap and stroked him lovingly, only it wasn't Spike, but a horrible, spitting stranger cat she'd never seen in her life. She dawdled off along the edge of the sea, collecting shells. She wasn't even going to think about that old sea enemy.

Tom found a piece of driftwood and wrote slogans in the soft clean sand. 'THE WONDERFUL ONE AND ONLY TOM BEANY,' he wrote. 'TOM BEANY SUPERSTAR.' Tom played in a band with Merv now, called The Night Kitchen. Sophie said they weren't too bad.

'Tilly – let's write a ginormous sand letter,' Tom called.

'I know – to the dolphins,' Tilly said at once, scuffing her way back to him through the shingle.

'What shall we say?' said Tom.

Tilly screwed up her eyes. 'Dear Dolphins,' she dictated at last. 'Help us save the world. It's too hard to do it on our own, that's why. Love and hugs from Tilly Beany aged six and three quarters.'

'You're nearly seven, Tilly, now, you know and I'm not sure about the hugs,' said Tom doubtfully. 'Anyway, computers are going to save the world, Merv says. Merv says computers are going to run the world by the end of this century. OK, OK,' he added, seeing Tilly's face. 'I'll do the writing. You decorate it with stuff.'

'I want to write "Tilly Beany" though,' said Tilly proudly. 'I can write "6" by myself but not " ³/4 ".'

Tom wouldn't put the hugs on in case someone saw him, so Tilly added tiny shell kisses just from her.

Kate came to admire their work. 'Are you sure dolphins can read human writing, Tilly?' she asked.

'Of course they can't,' said Tilly sternly. 'But they can read thoughts, didn't you know? When this letter washes into the sea, all the dolphins will know, even if they're far away.' She looked hard at Tom, but he was too busy popping bubbles on a piece of seaweed to notice. Then Tom said such a lovely thing that Tilly forgave him at once. 'Did you know, Tilly,' he said, 'that millions of years ago, everything on this beach including you, was once inside a star.'

Tilly's mouth dropped open.

'Honestly,' said Tom. 'All the tiny atoms your body is made of, used to be part of a star.'

'Oh, Tom,' said Tilly hugging him even though he was sandy. 'That's why I felt so tingly then! All those tiny atoms were homesick.'

As they were packing up to go and find a café for lunch, they heard someone calling. It was Aunt Rose. She had a crowd of ladies with her.

'Meet my favourite family,' Aunt Rose called to the ladies, picking her way down the shingle. 'I hoped we'd find you Beanys. Heavens, Tilly, last time I saw you, you were a mermaid with goosepimples.'

'Kate and I went to the loo in the night,' Tilly told her. 'We saw the stars.'

'My word,' said one of Aunt Rose's ladies. 'That's a sight isn't it? Gives me goosebumps every time.'

'Esme lives in Australia,' said Aunt Rose. 'She's

seen the stars out in the middle of the outback.'

'Not for a long time,' said Esme laughing. 'But I step into my little yard now and then and look up at the night sky and it's still amazing. Always changing, yet always the same. Like the sea.' Esme's brown eyes looked as if they were full of stories, sad stories as well as happy ones. She wore a dress with dotted patterns like little paths criss-crossing it. In and out of the paths darted leaping figures of animals and water creatures in such clear colours Tilly wanted to touch them.

'Your dress looks like a magic map,' said Tilly shyly.

'That's what it is, sweetheart,' said Esme. 'A special map that my people make, a dreamtime map. ' Esme's voice sounded like Australian people on TV when she spoke.

Tilly had never heard of a dreamtime map before. But the mysterious sounding word made her feel happily shivery the same way she did when Tom told her about belonging inside a star.

'What are those things with writing?' she asked.

'The placards? We've been on a march through town. We're holding a conference,' Aunt Rose explained. 'We want to make the world a better place for our grandchildren. We're all grannies, or old enough to be grannies. Esme has travelled thousands of miles to take part.'

'What do they say?' Tilly asked, peering at one of the placards.

'NO FORESTS – NO FUTURE,' said Esme, waving hers.

'GRANNIES OF THE WORLD UNITE AND FIGHT,' said a lady who looked too young to be anyone's granny. 'And now,' she said, unfastening the thin golden strap of her sandal, 'I'm going to paddle, if no one minds.'

Tilly couldn't imagine Grandma Susan paddling!

'Don't walk on our letter by mistake, please,' said Tilly anxiously.

'Letter?' The lady looked puzzled.

'In the sand,' said Tilly. 'It's to the dolphins.'

'A letter, eh?' said Esme. 'I'd like to see that if you don't mind, Tilly.'

But when the ladies reached the place where Tom and Tilly had written their letter, they didn't say a word.

'Did we do it wrong?' asked Tilly worried. 'I didn't know how to write " 3/4 " but Tom showed me.'

'No, it's beautiful, darling,' said the granny in the golden sandals, smiling.

'If you'll give us permission,' said Esme. 'I'll take a photograph to show my grandchildren in Australia.'

'Why don't you sign it too?' said Tom.

'Everyone can sign,' cried Tilly. 'The dolphins will know.'

'That's true,' said Esme seriously. 'Do you know, when I was a little girl, Tilly, my granny taught me a song for calling dolphins.'

Tilly almost stopped breathing. 'Did you call them?'

'Yes I did.'

'And did they come?'

'They came often.'

'Was it amazing? Like the stars? Always changing and always the same?' Tilly twisted her hands together with excitement.

'Yes,' said the old lady quietly. 'It was.' Then she put her arm round Tilly's shoulders, and murmured something and if anyone had been watching they would have seen Tilly's eyes go very round and green.

Then Esme said, 'Think you can remember that?'

And Tilly whispered, 'Yes.'

'That's the same way my granny taught me,' said Esme, smiling her sad happy smile.

Everyone signed their names in the wet sand. Some people decorated theirs with shells or pebbles. Several grannies took photographs. Then Aunt Rose said 'We hope you'll share our picnic.'

'We'd be honoured,' said Tilly's dad.

And even Sophie said, 'Cool.'

Tilly ate so many exciting kinds of food she was afraid she'd burst. Then, after the grannies had gone, she walked back down the beach.

The waves were nearly touching the grannies' names. In and out, they swished. Closer and closer. 'Tillee sssh – Tillee ssshh,' they whispered. As if they knew what Tilly was going to do.

She looked round to make sure no one was too near, then to make the charm specially strong she stretched her arms out wide and squeezed her eyes shut, the whole time she was singing Esme's song. She could feel her hair streaming back from her face and the salt wind stinging her skin.

Esme's dolphin charm was real dreamtime magic, Tilly knew.

So it was a terrible disappointment when she opened her eyes and saw nothing except the empty sea washing in and out. Nothing. Not even one little lost dolphin swimming up to the shore.

Sophie raced up. 'Tilly, guess what! We're

going rowing.'

Normally Tilly would be excited about going in a boat, but her head was too full of dolphin magic. 'I want to see what happens to our letter.'

'We can come back for supper,' said Sophie. 'We can have fish and chips on the beach, Dad says.'

'Is fish and chips vegetarian then?' asked Tilly.

Sophie tossed her hair. 'It's impossible to be vegetarian when you're camping.'

'Soph,' Tilly interrupted, because she had to tell someone, 'Esme taught me a dreamtime song for calling dolphins.'

'Cool,' said Sophie jealously. 'Wish she'd taught me.'

'But nothing happened,' said Tilly. Her lip quivered.

'Magic takes time,' Sophie reminded her.

But Tilly knew she must have done something wrong. Or why didn't the dolphins come?

Rowing was such hard work Dad had to buy ice-creams to help everyone recover. Then, after a walk through the heather, the Beanys drove back for supper.

'My hair feels stiff,' said Tilly.

'My skin smells of sea,' said Sophie sniffing the inside of her elbow.

'And I'm starvin' like Marvin,' said Tom.

Dad grinned. 'That's the seaside for you,' he said. 'I'm starvin' like Marvin too.'

Tilly's chips were too hot to eat fast. She had to keep licking her burnt fingers. The sun went sliding slowly down the sky, making a silky crimson path across the water.

But when she ran slithering along the shingle afterwards, there was no sign of the letter. This was the right place. She knew it was.

'The sea washed it away,' said Tilly in despair. 'The shells, the grannies' names. There's nothing left.'

'I thought that's what you wanted,' said Tom.

'It was,' said Tilly miserably.

But since she'd sung Esme's song she'd hoped for something truly, wonderfully magic.

'Come on, one last paddle,' said Sophie, pulling Tilly towards the sea.

'Wait for me, meanies,' yelled Kate laughing as

she grabbed Tilly's other hand, and they all went splashing into the sea.

'Oo-er, we're paddling in the actual dark!' said Tilly awed. 'Your dress looks ghosty white, Kate. Like moths.' Then she gasped. 'Sophie! Look!'

Sophie saw it at the same moment; a ghostly white stone flipping out of the darkening water on the curling edge of a wave. Kate caught it, then held it out without a word. Tilly couldn't speak either. The curving grey-white stone looked exactly like a dolphin. Esme's charm had worked. Tilly had a tiny dolphin of her very own.

'I can take this home and keep for ever can't I?' she said.

'For ever is a long time,' said Sophie, sounding like Mum.

'You can keep it now,' said Kate. 'That's what matters.'

'I liked those grannies,' Tilly whispered later,

snuggled between Kate and Sophie. 'When I'm old I'm going to wear golden sandals and a dress that's really a map. And I'll march to save the world.'

And she opened her hand secretly in the back of the car, showing Kate and Sophie her dolphin stone, gleaming like a little moon in the dusk.

'Yeah,' Sophie whispered back. 'The grannies were cool.'

5 Slowstars, glowstars

The day before Tilly's class was going to the planetarium, the worst thing happened. Just as Miss Hinchin started to read the going home story, Tilly was sick all down the twins. Both twins at the same time.

She hadn't been feeling sick. Though Tilly's mum did say she looked pale at breakfast time. And when they came indoors from afternoon play Miss Hinchin asked her if she felt all right, but Tilly said truthfully, 'I feel fine.' She was so excited about tomorrow's trip there wasn't enough room inside her for any new feelings.

Probably that's how the sick feeling sneaked in, like a mean old burglar. Tilly only had time to notice a strange taste in her mouth and the tiniest falling feeling in her tummy, when suddenly her lunch came roaring back out of her in the rudest way, all her peas, carrots and rice pudding whooshing horribly over Leena and Beena.

They jumped up shouting, 'Yuk, you horrible thing!'

Tilly was so shocked she jumped up too. Then she was sick again, on her own shoes this time.

It was worse than the worst dream Tilly ever had. Worse than the one about coming to school in her underwear. She didn't know what to do next, so she kept standing there for what felt like years, on legs that were suddenly too shivery to hold her up. The other children scrambled as far away from Tilly as they could.

But it wasn't a dream. It was real.

Leena and Beena were peering over their own shoulders, trying to wipe their sicky jumpers with pieces of paper towel. Miss Hinchin ran to fetch a bucket, saying, 'Try not to be sick again until I get back, Tilly,' as if Tilly had done it on purpose. Then she had to sit beside that horrible bucket outside Mrs Grosgrain's office, where everybody could see, until Mum came. Tilly thought she was going to die.

All the way home in the car she kept saying,

'I'll be better tomorrow, won't I?'

'I don't know,' Mum said sounding tired. 'Tom had this bug for days. Honestly, Tilly, why did you pick today to be ill? I've got a special meeting tomorrow. I've no idea who'll look after you. Sophie's got a clarinet exam and Kate's painting scenery for the school play. '

Mum beeped crossly as a van pulled out in front of her. 'Maybe I could find someone to look after you in the morning, then Tom could come straight home from the dentist's,' she murmured.

'You could always leave me all by myself,' said Tilly. Now Mum was behaving as if Tilly had been sick on purpose. Tilly was so hurt her voice wobbled. But Mum didn't notice. She was still busy thinking about babysitters.

'Maybe Emily's mum could sit with you,' Mum said. 'That's an idea.'

When they got home Mum tucked Tilly up on the sofa under the old picnic rug (with the washing-up bowl beside her in case) and dashed into the hall to make phone calls.

But Emily's mum had to take Ben to hospital tomorrow for new tests and Mum's other friends were busy. Tilly's dad was busy too.

Tilly pulled the rug up to her chin. The Beany's

living-room was growing bigger every minute. The bigger it grew, the lonelier Tilly felt all by herself on the sofa. She started to cry, hoping Mum would come to see what was the matter.

But Mum just went on nattering on the phone. No one came to say, 'Poor Tilly, you must feel really

sad.' No one came at all.

Tilly couldn't stand it. Tomorrow everyone except her was going to the planetarium to see how the stars and planets worked. She should be there too. She was part of a star, wasn't she? She pulled the rug right over her head and cried and cried.

'Tilly, why are you hiding by yourself in the dark.'

Kate snapped on the table lamp and peeled back Tilly's rug to find a shuddering, hiccuping little girl.

'Sweetheart, aren't you well?' Kate put her arms round her damp little sister.

'I was sick over the twins by mistake,' wept Tilly, blinking in the light like a baby owl. 'So I can't go to the planetarium. But no one cares anyway. No one w –'

'Listen, Tilly,' interrupted sensible Kate. 'Would you like a drink of lemon barley to sip? Only promise you'll stop if you feel even a tiny bit sick.'

'Yes, please, Kate,' said Tilly, leaning her hot cheek gratefully against Kate's cool shoulder.

'And when I come back, would you like a story?'

Yes, please, ' said Tilly. '"The Little Matchgirl" because . . .' Tilly's lip quivered again. New tears spilled down her face, '. . . because it's the saddest story I know.'

Tilly must have fallen asleep while Kate was reading. When she woke she was in her own bed. A slice of light fell softly through her open door. Spike was purring behind her knees, washing his paws so noisily it sounded as if he was eating really juicy oranges.

Tilly suddenly felt scared Spike might turn into that spitting stranger-cat the minute Mum switched off the landing light. She pushed him off the bed in a hurry and the little cat stalked off huffily to find Tom.

Then Tilly lay all by herself listening to Dad and Kate joking downstairs without her.

Her head hurt. Her bedcovers felt strange too, as if they might float up to the ceiling if they felt like it. Tilly didn't feel like the usual Tilly any more. She didn't feel like someone who used to belong to a star. She felt like a little lost balloon bumping against the walls in the dark.

When she woke again it was morning. Mum was pulling back her curtains. Mum had her smart suit on and some strappy new shoes. When she sat on Tilly's bed, lovely perfume floated round Tilly like a soothing cloud.

'Feeling better, Tilly?' Mum asked. 'Sorry I was crabby yesterday. I was so worried what to do about you. But Emily's mum said Uncle Dolphus will stay with you till Tom gets back. He says if you need anything, call him. OK?'

'Oh,' said Tilly sitting up in such a rush she felt dizzy again. But before she could say no, it wasn't

OK to be left with a strange uncle she'd never seen before in her life, Tilly's mum whisked out of the room again. Then she popped her head back in, beaming.

'I'll bring you back something special, promise.'

'Oh,' said Tilly, lying down again.

Maybe she could make herself go back to sleep until Tom came back. Then the uncle could go home again and Tom could help her make a special telephone for talking to children on faraway planets. Tilly had been planning to make that telephone ever since she saw *ET*, and now she knew for sure that she probably had some actual relations in outer space . . .

But however hard she thumped her pillow and tried to get comfy, Tilly didn't feel a bit sleepy.

'I'll draw a spaceship ark,' she decided. 'I'll make a list of everyone who's allowed on it and the things we need to take. Bernice can't come anyway.'

She went hunting around her room, on legs that felt new and wobbly, like Bambi's. Then she remembered. Her crayons were in the kitchen. Maybe if she tiptoed downstairs quietly the uncle wouldn't hear her. Tilly crept downstairs in her bare feet. Suddenly, on the bottom step, she froze.

What if Emily's uncle appeared in the doorway, just as she was going past.

So she called in a casual voice, 'I'm just getting my drawing things, all right? But I don't need anything, thanks.'

And a voice called back, 'That's fine, man. No problem.'

The uncle's voice was a surprise. Quiet, deep and dreamy.

Tilly scurried into the kitchen, grabbed her drawing things and scuttled back. Then, just as she was going back upstairs, she had a peep through the living-room door.

But all she could see was the back of a newspaper and a pair of long, long legs jutting out. Emily's uncle must be a giant, Tilly decided.

Then she noticed Emily's uncle's shoes. She knew they'd have to be big to match those mile long legs. What surprised her was how shiny they were. They weren't shiny and hard, like new shoes just out of the box. These were very old shoes, but polished so silky soft they looked friendly, almost smiley. Tilly wanted to stroke one. Uncle Dolphus must love those shoes to take such good care of them.

'When I've done my drawing, I might show it to you,' she called cautiously.

'Well now, is that right?' said Uncle Dolphus in the same deep dreamy voice.

Tilly skipped back upstairs with her crayons. Her legs weren't so wobbly now. She drew a beautiful ark. She put a glass ceiling in the bedrooms so people could look at the stars while they were going to sleep. And she put in a little indoor garden with a fountain to cheer everyone up on their long journey to the new planet, which was so new it didn't even have a name yet. Then she made a list of the things the Beanys would need to take with them. Vegetarian food for one thing. It wouldn't be very friendly to save all the animals, then cook them for dinner as soon as everyone got hungry.

Actually, Tilly realised, she was hungry now. Very, very hungry.

She pattered back downstairs.

'Mum forgot to give me breakfast,' she said to Emily's uncle's shoes. 'I can get everything out of the cupboards but I'm not allowed to use the toaster because it sticks.'

'I wouldn't mind a cup of coffee myself, man,' said Uncle Dolphus, putting down his paper. 'Lead the way.'

Uncle Dolphus looked more like a grandad than an uncle. There were silvery tufts in his hair. His eyes were the smiley kind, Tilly noticed.

'Hello, Uncle Dolphus,' said Tilly, now she could see all of him.

'Hello, Miss Beany,' said Uncle Dolphus very seriously, just as if Tilly was a grown-up. Emily's daddy did that too.

'The kitchen's this way,' said Tilly. 'But I'm not a man, didn't you know?' she told him, giggling. 'I'm a girl.'

'In Jamaica we call everyone "man",' said Uncle Dolphus following her. 'Boys, girls, women.'

Uncle Dolphus didn't stoop like an old person, Tilly noticed. He moved gracefully like a tall calm bird who has all the time in the world to get where it's going.

'Is Jamaica where you live?' said Tilly, fetching the coffee jar down for him.

'It is,' said Uncle Dolphus. 'See this big red jumper Carrie knitted for me now? It's the first time I ever had to wear such a heavy great thing in my life. And you know what? I'm scared to take it off. It's supposed to be summer here and already the cold is enough to kill me. Man, I miss that Jamaican sunshine. I miss it fiercely, in here you know.' Uncle Dolphus tapped his chest. Tilly never saw such a serious face as Emily's Uncle's before in her life. It was just his shoes and eyes that were smiley.

'How long have you been here then?' said Tilly.

'Just a month or so,' said Uncle Dolphus vaguely. 'Visiting relations, you know, before I get too old for gadding about.'

Uncle Dolphus made hot drinks for them both and whisked the toast out of the toaster exactly one second before it started to burn, the way Tilly told him.

'Is it always hot in Jamaica?' Tilly asked,

carrying her buttered toast carefully to the table.

'Except when it rains,' said Uncle Dolphus. 'And even then, the air smells so sweet. Imagine the most beautiful garden you could ever dream of. Ah, man, it smells even more beautiful than that. ' He closed his eyes as if he was homesick already.

'Oh,' breathed Tilly, clutching the honey jar, feeling giddy with homesickness herself. Perhaps part of her had once belonged to Jamaica as well as belonging to a star. 'Why does it smell so sweet?'

'Some of it is the plants that grow on the island,' explained Uncle Dolphus. 'Some of it is the food we cook. Yam and callaloo, fried chicken, rice and peas. The smell of roasting breadfruit, now that's a kind of smoky sweet smell. Makes me hungry just to think of it.'

'Have some of my toast,' said Tilly kindly. 'You made loads.'

'Sure you can manage that jar?' said Uncle Dolphus.

Tilly nodded. 'I should have gone to the planetarium today,' she told him. 'But I was sick down the twins.'

'That old planetarium is nothing, believe me,' said Uncle Dolphus comfortably sipping his coffee. 'Wait till you see the stars come out in Jamaica. Bright! Brighter than your eyes, Miss Beany. Even the darkness in Jamaica is brighter than anywhere else. Oh it's dark all right. But still kind of bright too. Like something alive, you know?'

'Amazing,' said Tilly, trying to imagine stars brighter than the ones she'd seen with Kate.

'And the same time the stars come out, the crickets and tree frogs start to make their sweet-sweet night music. You know, until I was old enough to know better, I used to think the stars were singing.'

'Are you really Emily's uncle?' Tilly asked shyly.

'Strictly speaking, I'm Paul's grandfather's brother,' Uncle Dolphus explained. 'His "gran-uncle", we say in Jamaica. But Paul grew up in my house, Tilly, and I love him as much as if he was my son. That's one reason I'm here. To check on how he's getting on.'

'I've got one grandma. That's all my relations I've got, on this planet anyway,' said Tilly. 'We have to call her Susan. She's pretty, like a film star, but she can't do anything in case she ruins her tights. And she gets headaches,' Tilly added gloomily.

'Your grandma just needs her loving family all around her,' said Uncle Dolphus, nodding. 'Then her headaches will simply melt away.' He started humming to himself.

'Tilly didn't know how to explain that it was Grandma Susan's loving family that gave her the headaches in the first place. It usually took her an hour after she arrived before she'd even unbutton her coat and put down her handbag.

'You ever hear Paul sing, Tilly?' Uncle Dolphus said unexpectedly.

'Emily's daddy? Never,' said Tilly astonished. 'Well, maybe once,' she remembered. 'He was fixing his van in the rain. But he stopped singing when he saw me coming.'

'Paul was the best singer in Spanish Town,' said Uncle Dolphus. 'All the girls in our church fall down in a dead faint when he start to sing, you know. That man work so hard now, all the music drain clean out of him. It break my heart.'

'They want to send Ben somewhere to learn to walk,' said Tilly. 'That's why their daddy works so hard. Emily told me.'

'Best singer in Spanish Town,' repeated Uncle Dolphus stubbornly. He cleared his throat. 'So, Tilly, tell me something about yourself now, man.'

Tilly licked the dribbles of honey off her fingers. Grown-ups didn't usually ask her to talk. And it was wonderful talking to Uncle Dolphus. But she wanted him to go on talking about Jamaica. Tilly could listen to Uncle Dolphus for hours. 'I know, let's take turns,' she said, creeping nearer to Uncle Dolphus's chair. 'First me talking, then you.'

So Tilly told Uncle Dolphus about how hard it was to be the ordinary Tilly Beany when she started school, and how Kate's old dancing teacher, Miss Violet Gladwell, helped when she'd got stuck being Cindertilly. Then she told about when Bernice didn't want to be her best friend and how she invented the Best Friend Machine. 'I've got Emily, Nessa and Beth now,' she told Uncle Dolphus. 'I've got loads of friends now.'

'I can see you're the kind of girl who makes

things happen,' Uncle Dolphus said, chuckling.

'That's true, because, do you know, now we're going to save the world,' said Tilly excitedly. 'At the beach there were some grannies with placards but Tom says science is the best way. Miss Gladwell's sister was ill and medicine made her well again. Medicine is science, isn't it?'

Uncle Dolphus looked thoughtful. 'Well, Miss Beany, once you've got this little world-saving project under control, see if you can persuade my nephew to sing for you some time. That would really make me happy.'

'Tell me about when you were little, ' said Tilly, leaning against Uncle Dolphus's chair, closing her eyes so she could hear his deep, quiet voice better.

So Uncle Dolphus told her how he and his sisters had to carry water home in pails, because there were no water pipes in the houses then. 'No electricity either,' said Uncle Dolphus. 'Sometimes, if my sisters wanted to read or sew after sunset, they'd catch fireflies. Insects like sparks of firelight, Tilly. We'd put them in a jar and use the firefly light to see by. Another time, I remember, we were hungry and my sisters and I begged my mother to cook us ackee and salt fish for our Sunday breakfast. But it was too early in the season. Our ackee tree wasn't ready yet. Ackee looks a bit like scrambled eggs when it's cooked,' Uncle Dolphus explained, seeing Tilly's puzzled expression. 'It tastes delicious, believe me. So my mother now, she tell us to go and stand under the ackee tree and laugh, yes, laugh. As loud and long as we could. She tell us that the laughter of little children is the only thing in the world, apart from God's sunlight, that can ripen ackee.'

'Did it work?' asked Tilly, hardly breathing.

'Do you know, I don't even remember,' said

Uncle Dolphus shaking his head. 'All I remember is me and my sisters in our Sunday clothes, standing under that ackee tree, laughing till our sides hurt .'

'Did your mum tell you stories?' Tilly asked.

'My granny used to tell Anansi stories,' said Uncle Dolphus. 'About a spider who was always tricking the other animals. '

'Better not tell Emily,' said Tilly. 'She hates creepy-crawlies.'

'Sometimes, when everyone's work was done, she and my grandfather and my other aunts and uncles would teach us old songs and dances that were handed down from African times.'

'African times?' asked Tilly puzzled again. 'I thought you lived in Jamaica.'

Uncle Dolphus wasn't listening. 'In Jamaica no one's too young to dance and no one's too old. Any time of day or night, music is thumping out somewhere, like the strongest heartbeat you ever heard.' He stared into space, dreamily tapping out a rhythm on the arm of the chair.

'Tell me some more,' said Tilly greedily.

But Uncle Dolphus was miles away.

'Uncle Dolphus is an unusual name isn't it?' Tilly said, desperate for him to go on talking to her. 'It sounds like "dolphin".'

'Plenty of strange names in my country,' said Uncle Dolphus softly. 'It start in slavery times, after we were stolen out of Africa, then we kind of keep up the tradition all by ourselves.'

Tilly wanted to ask him more about that, but something in Uncle Dolphus's eyes made her stop. She guessed slavery was one of those big grown-up sadnesses that was too hard to understand, like hungry children and holes in the sky and beautiful rainforests that were gone for ever. Then, before she could say anything else, Tom came banging in the kitchen door smelling of the dentists, and it was time for Uncle Dolphus to go.

'Visit me as soon as you're well again, Miss Beany,' said Uncle Dolphus, 'and I'll cook you cornmeal porridge with cinnamon leaf in it. It's the best thing in the world for building up your strength.'

'Cornmeal porridge,' said Tom, laughing, when Uncle Dolphus had gone. 'Whatever's that?'

'You don't know anything, do you Tom Beany?' said Tilly furiously. 'You don't even know what an ackee tree is, so there. Only two things can ripen ackee fruit, you know. God's sunlight and the laughter of little children. So ha-ha to you!'

And she slammed the door and marched

upstairs, stamping as hard as she could on every stair.

'Well, what did I say?' Tom asked himself.

Soon afterwards Mum came home. Her meeting finished earlier than she thought.

'Guess what I've brought you?' said Mum, flinging open Tilly's door. 'Your own private planetarium. Ta-da!' She threw Tilly a big rustling brown paper bag.

'Glowstars!' shouted Tilly. I've wanted these my whole life! Help me stick them up, Tom.'

'So we're speaking now, are we?' grinned Tom.

'Actually they'll be more like *slowstars*,' Mum said. 'They won't glow until it's really dark. Anyway, how did you get on with Uncle Dolphus?'

'Don't ask her,' Tom advised her. 'She'll slam doors and shout.'

Mum raised her eyebrows.

'No I won't,' scowled Tilly. 'He told me stories that's all.'

Because she couldn't explain that she secretly

wished Uncle Dolphus was her relation, instead of Grandma Susan, who just talked about TV programmes and how Mum used the wrong soap powder. Mum would be hurt.

Late that night, Tilly heard Kate tiptoe past her door.

'Hello Kate,' she whispered.

'Still awake, Tilly?' said Kate. 'Oh, isn't your ceiling fantastic!'

'The planet with the rings is Saturn, Tom says,' whispered Tilly. 'Tom's going to give us some science things so me, Emily and everyone can be famous scientists when I'm well.'

'Clever you,' said Kate. She'd just cycled back from her play rehearsal. Her hair smelled like a summery meadow. 'It's your birthday soon,' she reminded Tilly. 'Mum says you can have a party if you like.'

'Kate,' said Tilly. 'Have you heard of ackee trees?'

'Never,' said Kate. 'What are they?'

'I don't know,' said Tilly. 'Uncle Dolphus and his sisters had to laugh under one before they could have breakfast.'

'Your face is still hot,' said Kate, stroking her cheek.

'Kate,' said Tilly, kicking off her crumpled sheet,

gazing up at her starry, mysterious ceiling.

'Yes?'

'You've never ever once seen fireflies either have you?'

'Never ever once,' said Kate smiling.

'They look like sparks of fire,' said Tilly dreamily. 'Uncle Dolphus's sisters put them in a jar so they had enough light to sew by.'

Kate smoothed Tilly's damp hair with her cool meadow-smelling hand. 'Starlight, starbright,' she sang softly. 'First star I see tonight.'

Tilly started singing too, the one about putting a star in your pocket. Grandma Susan taught her that song. That was one thing about Grandma, she remembered good songs. Then Tilly started making up her own song. 'Slowstars, glowstars.' And she wondered if glowstars counted for wishing on.

'Kate,' she said sleepily, 'did you know Emily's daddy was the best singer in Spanish Town? Man, when he started singing, all the girls in the church used to fall in a dead fain –'

Tilly's eyelids flickered and closed.

But Kate stayed where she was and a minute later Tilly opened her eyes again. 'Anyway, Kate,' she said chattily, 'Uncle Dolphus was heaps better than that stupid old planetarium.'

'Night-night, Tilly,' said Kate softly. 'Starry dreams.'
But Tilly was really asleep this time.

6 The butterfly hat

As soon as Tilly was well, she went round to Emily's house to tell her they were going to be famous scientists. But when Emily's dad let her in, Tilly heard Ben screaming upstairs.

'What's the matter with Ben?' asked Tilly.

'He had some tests at the hospital yesterday,' said Emily's dad in a tired voice. 'That always makes him crabby. He woke up at four this morning and hasn't stopped yelling since.'

'Poor old Ben,' said Tilly sympathetically.

'And poor old us,' said Emily's dad.

Emily was on the sofa in her dressing-gown.

'Come on sleepy-head,' Tilly said. 'We've got to start doing science right away if we're going to be famous. Some people have a boring chemistry set they get from a shop, but it's better to invent your own private chemicals.' She patted the old schoolbag slung across her tummy. 'I've brought millions of science stuff. A ruler with stencils Tom gave me. A rubber tube. Jars and labels, so we can put the name of our new invention on the jars.'

'What are we going to invent anyway, Tilly?' asked Emily.

'We won't know yet,' said Tilly. 'No one knows what they're inventing before they do it.'

'Science usually explodes, doesn't it?' said Emily, chewing her thumb in a worried way.

'Only sometimes,' said Tilly calmly. 'But we'll make sure Spike is indoors so we don't blow him up by mistake.'

'Are we doing the science outside then?'

'Yes,' said Tilly. 'Because one thing about science – it has to smell terrible, or it won't work!'

'Ugh, pooh,' said Emily. She ran off to get dressed, giggling.

Emily's dad came downstairs with Ben who was still crying.

'What's the matter, Benjamin Bunny?' Tilly asked.

Ben scowled. 'Not your bunny.'

'We thought he'd had a bad dream,' sighed Ben's dad. 'But probably it's because my Uncle Dolphus went away to my brother's for a day or two.'

'Na-oow,' screamed Ben. Then he started shouting something that sounded like 'barf eye at dreeb.'

'What's that mean, you funny boy?' asked Tilly trying not to laugh. 'Bath fly mat dreeb?'

'Na-oow!' yelled Ben even more angrily.

Emily's dad shook his head. 'He keeps screaming the same thing. Even Emily can't understand him.'

'Hmmn,' said Tilly thoughtfully.

And she picked up Ben's special telephone and punched its buttons.

'Dring-ring,' it went.

Ben was so surprised he took a big wobbly

breath. Before he could start shouting again Tilly
held out the phone.

'It's for you,' she said.

Ben took it. 'Who's zat?' he said sadly. One long
wiggly tear slid down his cheek.

'The dream shop lady,' said Tilly into her hand,
in her shop lady voice. 'Can you help me, please?'

Ben scowled again 'I carn help you, lady,' he
said into the phone. 'I'm only little.'

'Oh,' said the dream lady surprised. 'Aren't you
the boy who's been screaming ever since he
borrowed one of our dreams?' Ben looked more
surprised than ever. 'Yus?' he said.

'You see, last night we rented out some new
dreams, but the labels got mixed up. We're worried
some little boy might have got a nightmare

intended for teenage viewers. Did you borrow a horrible dream by mistake, Ben?'

'No-o, not 'orrible,' said Ben. Another tear slid down his nose. 'It was nice an' lovely,' he said. Then he threw down his phone, covered his face and cried.

'Ben's upset because he had a really magicky dream,' said the dream lady to Emily's dad, in Tilly's voice. 'Once I tried to get back into a lovely flying dream, but it was time to get up.'

Emily's dad looked even more tired now. 'A dream is just a dream,' he said. 'When it's over it's gone for ever. It's not real.'

Tilly knew he was wrong. Dreams were a different kind of real, that's all. Underneath the ordinary world, Tilly could always feel the world of dreams tugging and whispering like invisible tides. Probably Ben felt that way too, because Ben and Tilly were birthday twins.

Her birthday twin was kicking on the floor now, yelling. 'Gone! Barfly dreeb gone!'

'Ben, stop this and come and have breakfast,' said Emily's dad.

'No breakfas'. No, don' want it!' Ben wailed into the carpet. 'Want my barfly dreeb.'

When Tilly was little no one understood how

she felt inside either. They just saw her small ordinary outside. Ben wasn't three yet. He couldn't talk well enough to tell people about the dreams inside his head.

'Listen, Ben,' Tilly said. 'Can you do me a painting of your lovely dream?'

Ben stopped yelling. 'Why?' he said tearily, but he sounded a tiny bit interested.

'Because I want to borrow that dream next, silly,' said Tilly.

'Oh,' said Ben snuffling. 'I jus' get my paints, awright, Tilly.' He scooted off, hiccupping sadly, his hair sticking up like little ruffled question marks.

'Mum's given us some food colouring,' said Emily, bouncing in. 'And here's my pocket-money sherbert. Science is mostly fizzy isn't it?'

Tilly absolutely loved sherbert. 'We don't want the science to turn out too fizzy, Em,' she said wickedly. 'We might have to eat a *leetle* bit.'

Emily giggled. 'Naughty Tilly! Let's get Beth.'

But Beth had the same horrible sickness bug Tilly had, so they went to Nessa's house. Nessa's mum gave them some cooking soda, and two whole trays of ice cubes.

'It's a good thing we've got this ice,' said Tilly as they went back to her house. 'Because if the science gets too hot and we want to stop it exploding, we can cool it down really fast.'

'That's what I thought,' said Nessa.

'Don't we need a big black pot to boil the science in?' Emily asked.

'That's for spells, silly,' giggled Nessa. 'You have test-tubes to do science. But Tilly, don't we need to wait until there's some lightning?'

Tilly frowned. 'What for?' she asked.

'I don't know what for, ' said Nessa. 'I think it's just there, outside the window at the same time as you do the science.'

'I don't think you have to have lightning,' said Tilly at last. 'Except when you're making a horrible monster come alive.'

'Oh, I remember,' said Nessa puffing out her cheeks. 'So we don't need lightning, then.'

'No,' said Tilly. 'We aren't doing the monster kind of science. '

'We aren't, are we?' said Nessa.

Tilly, Emily and Nessa had a wonderful morning doing science in Tilly's garden. When Sophie came to see how they were getting on, they were stirring jars of sludgy liquid with some useful sticks Tilly had found in Mum's greenhouse.

'You know what would make your experiment

really gungy,' Sophie said.

'No, what, Soph?' said Tilly at once.

'That torn-up newspaper you left in a bucket weeks ago when you wanted to make paper and save trees.'

'Oh, I forgot that!' said Tilly excitedly.

So they put the soggy newspaper in too.

'We've got to stir it really well,' said Tilly.

They stirred till their arms ached.

'Oo-er, my ice cubes are melting,' Nessa said. 'That means our science is getting hot, hot, HOT!'

Emily pinched her nose. 'Does your jar smell terrible enough yet, Tilly?' she said. 'I think mine does.'

'Don't worry,' said Tilly, trying not to breathe. 'The science smells really real now.'

Some nasturtium petals blew down from one of Tilly's mum's hanging baskets. Tilly tossed one whole pepper-smelling petal in each jar, because she suddenly felt absolutely sure the science needed them.

'This is very strong science,' she said, closing her eyes. 'And did you know, it's called – The Cure For Everything. I'm going to write that on my label.'

'So am I,' said Nessa at once. 'And we're going to give some to Beth to make her better, aren't we?'

Emily's dad came through the gate then, with Ben riding on his shoulders. Ben was waving a painty sheet of paper.

'Sorry to interrupt, ladies,' said Emily's dad.

'Oh – Ben's dream,' Tilly remembered.

She put down her stirring stick, and carefully took the painting out of Ben's red-and-blue painty hand.'

'What a lovely painting, Ben,' said Nessa brightly. 'What is it meant to be?'

'My barfly dreeb, silly,' said Ben, hiccupping.

Tilly gazed silently into the swirls and squiggles of Ben's painting.

'My lovely barfly 'at zat is,' said Ben sadly. 'You know, Tilly.'

Tilly began to smile. 'This is you, Ben, isn't it?' She pointed to a fat blue circle with spidery arms and legs.

Ben nodded. 'Yus. Zat me.'

'And this er – this must be your beautiful – er hat?' she suggested hopefully, pointing to a gold crinkly dish-shape, floating above the blue circle.

'Yus!' shouted Ben, all smiles now, 'My 'at wiv barflies. Zat my barfly 'at! Zat my special chair too,' he added.

'Chair?' said Tilly, baffled. This was the first time Emily's brother had mentioned a chair in his dream.

'Barfly prince chair,' Ben explained beaming, drumming his fingers on his daddy's head.

'Hey, Benjamin, you're meant to be kind to the poor old horse, you know,' said his dad.

Ben hadn't said anything about princes either.

'Do you mean "throne"?' Tilly asked him. 'Usually princes have thrones.'

'Yus,' agreed Ben. 'Barfly vrone.'

Tilly went on staring at the crinkly gold dish. 'But what are those funny little sweetie papers?' Then, all at once, she saw. 'Ben, this is you being a prince on a throne, wearing your butterfly hat – probably he means crown,' she explained to the others.

'Butterfly hat?' said Emily's dad amazed. 'Is that what you've been shouting all morning, Ben?'

'Yus,' said Ben happily, nodding his head so hard Tilly thought he'd nod it right off. 'Been shoutin' "barflies", I have. "BARFLY PRINCE", I been sayin'!'

'So we just have to make Ben a butterfly hat, I mean crown, so he can be a butterfly prince and he'll be happy,' said Tilly cheerfully. 'Kate can help. She's brilliant at dressing-up things.'

Ben was laughing now. 'Thank you, Tilly! Lovely barflies on my 'at. '

He zigzagged his hands through the air, opening and closing his fingers like wings. 'Lovely real barflies on my prince's 'at.'

Tilly's smile vanished. 'Real butterflies? Are you sure they were real ones, Ben?' she asked.

'Yus, real barflies,' said Ben, still happily fluttering his hands. 'Going to get my barfly 'at now, Tilly?'

'Don't be silly, Ben,' said Ben's dad gently. 'That was just a dream. How in the world can Tilly get you a real butterfly hat?'

Ben's mouth turned itself into a letterbox shape, ready for more screaming.

'It's all right,' said Tilly quickly. 'I just wanted to

be sure what kind of butterfly hat Ben wanted. Real ones take longer to organise,' she murmured. 'But they're always worth it. Always.'

'Are we doing some more science this afternoon?' asked Nessa at lunch-time.

'No,' said Tilly thoughtfully. 'I'm going to be busy.'

And she went indoors where Kate's boyfriend Ollie was making toast.

'Do you want your beans on your toast or beside your toast, Tilly?' asked Kate.

'Mmmn,' said Tilly dreamily. 'Please, Kate.'

'Oops,' said Ollie. ' Some little witch or a pirate with a dangerous moustache is going to turn up any minute.' Ollie didn't know Tilly when she turned into all those other Tillies, but Kate had told him lots of stories.

'No,' said Tilly's dad, smiling at Tilly. 'Tilly's a reformed character. Though her eyes do look very green in this light.'

Tilly ate three beans very slowly to show everyone she was still the real Tilly Beany. Then she had a drink of milk and carefully wiped away her milk moustache before she said, 'It's about my birthday, because I do want a party after all and it's a very amazing surprise, but you've got to help me anyway. '

'I think you'd better explain more about this amazing surprise first, Tilly, before we actually sign anything,' said Tilly's dad laughing.

So Tilly explained and everyone was truly astonished, the way she knew they would be.

'That is an amazing idea, Tilly,' said Kate.

'I can't promise, Jellybean,' said Tilly's dad. 'But I might know a man who knows a man.'

'But what does that mean, Daddy?' asked Tilly in despair .

'It means he'll try to help,' said Sophie's friend Rose quickly. 'Can I come, Tilly?'

'Yes,' said Tilly. 'Everyone's coming. Even catty old Bernice. But it's a HUGE secret.' She put her finger to her lips.

Ollie zipped his mouth shut. 'OK, boss,' he whispered.

In the end Tilly's dad must have found a man who knew a man, because he said Tilly could actually have her amazing surprise party!

After lunch on the day of the party Tilly went to find Emily. 'My mum says, are you nearly ready?' she asked.

'Ye-es,' said Emily. 'But why aren't we having

the party at your house, Tilly?'

'Because this is more special,' said Tilly. 'And guess what? Tom's band is going to play some music for – you know who, Em,' and she and Em giggled together in a secret sort of way, before Tilly went on, 'and Rose and Sophie are going to be dancing girls!'

'Sophie?' said Emily amazed. 'Dancing?'

'Here's the map for your Mum and Dad. The arrows are the way you have to drive and the big X is where the party is. '

'Like a pirate map,' said Emily giggling. 'But why has Ben got to come? He'll yell and spoil everything.'

'He won't yell at this party,' promised Tilly mysteriously. 'Uncle Dolphus is coming, isn't he?'

'He's made himself look so smart he says you'll fall down in a dead faint when you see him,' said Emily. 'Tilly, I'm so excited, I've got butterflies.'

But for some reason this sent Tilly off into fits of giggles.

'I don't see why your mother couldn't drive you herself and leave me out of this,' Emily's dad grumbled as he drove his big van along the little lanes. 'I was planning to put up some shelves this weekend.'

'Tilly said you had to be at this party, Dad,' said Emily. 'She said it wouldn't be the same without you.' She winked at Uncle Dolphus. Uncle Dolphus winked back and started humming a little tune. Emily squashed her hankie into her mouth. She knew why Tilly wanted her dad at the party. So did Uncle Dolphus. But it was a big secret.

'Children's parties,' said Emily's dad frowning in his driving mirror. 'Jelly and pass-the-parcel. Huh! I can't believe I let you talk me into this.'

But Emily knew her dad was just shy.

'Heavens,' said Emily's mum. 'Tilly isn't having the party here, is she?'

She gazed in astonishment at the grand old house amongst the trees. 'Doesn't some old lord live there?'

'It's a muscum now,' said Emily's dad. 'Hey, someone's tied ribbons to the trees to show us where to park.'

'There's Tilly waving,' shouted Emily. 'What's that building, Mum? It looks like a funny little palace.'

'Some kind of old-fashioned greenhouse,' said Emily's mum. 'What a peculiar place for a party.'

'Oh, I see Tilly now!' said Ben.

'Hello everyone!' shouted Tilly. 'Put on these special things.'

'Miss Beany what are you up to?' said Emily's dad sighing. 'How come I let you and my little daughter here go hijacking my weekend plans for this birthday foolishness.'

'Don't mind him, Tilly,' said Emily's mum. 'What are these special things you've got for us?'

'Your beautiful party hats!' said Tilly. 'Your ones are crowns anyway because you're the royal guests.' And then Tilly went into another mysterious fit of giggles.

Ollie appeared, wearing an apron over his trousers like a servant from the olden days, except he was holding one of those plastic bottles for spraying plants. 'You have to spray the crowns with this or the birthday magic won't work,' he told them. And he sprayed the golden birthday crowns with something wet.

Emily's dad put his crown on, but looked as if he was secretly planning to take it off again as soon as no one was looking and put his favourite cap back on.

'And now, your Majesties,' said Ollie, making a bow, 'Follow me.'

'Oh, I can hear music,' said Emily's dad cheering up suddenly. 'Not bad either.'

'Me too,' said Uncle Dolphus winking at Emily again.

'Our special singer couldn't come though,' said Tilly pulling a sad face. 'I don't know what we're going to do.'

'What's going on?' asked Emily's dad suspiciously. 'I wasn't born yesterday, you know, Miss Beany.'

But Ollie was placing the smallest, most beautiful crown of all on Ben's soft curly hair.

Ben reached up wonderingly to touch it. Then he froze in astonishment.

Inside the greenhouse, bright little scraps of colour flittered amongst tangled stems, or rested on sun-dappled leaves.

Ben didn't smile or shout when he saw them. He looked like a sleepwalker who's been shocked awake.

Uncle Dolphus was more excited than Ben. 'Lord have mercy,' he said. 'What kind of crazy party you brought me to?'

Now they were all inside the sunlit glass palace, breathing in warm steamy air which smelled sweeter than the flower-shop. Then the door closed again, and suddenly butterflies were everywhere, white, blue, chalky green, turquoise, orange, gold. Some had wings edged with flame or ebony. Some were speckled; some were plain.

The party guests stepped back and Ben saw the chair Ollie and Kate had decorated with painted butterflies and piled high with tasselled cushions, so it looked exactly like a magic throne.

Ben reached his hand up to touch the glittering edges of his crown again. He looked at the waiting people.

A little girl in a party dress waved at him. 'Hello, Ben,' she said.

Ben took off his crown, staring at it in a worried way, as though he had no idea what it was doing on his head.

That's when Tilly nearly burst out crying.

After all her plans, Ben hated her amazing idea. He hated being her birthday-party twin. He hated the painted crowns and the magic throne. He hated the butterfly house with its rainbow-coloured butterflies softly zigzagging through the air. Probably he'd hate the butterfly birthday cakes too, one for him and one for Tilly. Tilly'd never felt so disappointed in her life.

Suddenly Ben stuck his crown back on.

'What's he saying, Tilly?' someone asked.

Ben's face was still serious, the way a butterfly prince ought to look, but his eyes were shining. And he was saying huskily, 'Are the barflies on my prince's 'at, yet, Tilly? Are they?'

And Tilly breathed out a shivery sigh. It was all right!

Everyone smiled as the cloud of tiny blue butterflies settled on Ben's crown at last, attracted by the sugar mixture Ollie had sprayed there. And Emily's dad secretly hid his crown behind a big bush and put his favourite cap back on.

'Yes,' said Tilly softly, 'you're a real butterfly prince now, Ben.'

'And now,' shouted Tom, 'Ben and Tilly's Butterfly Birthday Party can begin.'

And it did. Everyone said it was the most amazing party they'd been to.

'Butterflies aren't creepy-crawlies, Tilly, are they?' Emily whispered.

'No,' said Tilly firmly. 'They're completely different.'

And halfway through the party, Miss Gladwell came in, wearing her swishy long skirt and tip-tapping shoes. Tilly was so surprised and pleased she couldn't even say one word.

'Look, Tilly!' yelled Emily. She'd taken off her shoes and socks so Ollie could spray her toes with sugar water. 'I'm going to have a butterfly slipper and I'm not scared.'

'That's Emily,' explained Tilly. 'Her daddy didn't want to sing but Miss Hinchin and Uncle Dolphus said he had to.'

'Hello, lady,' said Ben from under his lopsided crown of butterflies. He waved a half-eaten sandwich. 'Look at my lovely barfly hat!'

Miss Violet Gladwell gazed around her at the tropical flowers and vines; at Emily with her butterfly slipper, at Sophie and Kate in their dancing girl clothes, at Uncle Dolphus with baby Maya on his knee, and at Emily's dad pushing his cap to the back of his head. And she began to smile.

'Happy birthday, Tilly Beany,' she said. 'But before I give you your present, tell me one thing. Have you kept those storms and rainbows safe inside you all this time?'

Instead of answering, Tilly hugged Miss Gladwell tightly round her middle. Then she said, 'My other friends are Beth and Nessa and we're going to save the world, anyway.' But she said it in a whisper.

Because just then Emily's dad tipped back his head and right in the middle of Tilly and Ben's Butterfly Birthday Party, he began to sing.

7 Tilly saves the world

Tilly was so tired after her party, she fell asleep before her head touched the pillow.

The night air blew in softly through the curtains. With it drifted the sweet peppery smell of summer flowers. A warm wind stirred Tilly's hair. The moonlight moved across her bed until it was shining right in her eyes .

'All right moon,' said Tilly sleepily. 'I'm coming.'

And without putting on her slippers, Tilly slipped out of the open window into the darkness, and floated gently down into the yard.

Behind the broken broom and the rain barrel, exactly where she'd left it, she found The Cure For Everything. And though her eyes weren't used to the dark yet, it seemed to her the moonlight had changed the cure in some way.

It didn't smell so terrible for one thing. It smelled lovely. Even nicer than Mum's hand-cream. Then, because the moon was still calling and calling her, Tilly flew up into the sky, carefully holding her jar.

She went higher than she'd ever flown in a dream before, but she wasn't scared because she could hear Naomi's moon chimes in the apple tree.

Up above the roofs and chimney pots she flew, high over the lights of the town. And, as Tilly flew, she felt the starlight tingling in the ends of her hair as if the stars were reminding her that long, long ago Tilly and the stars belonged to the same family. And now and then, through the moon chimes, she could actually hear the stars too, singing their sweet-sweet night music, like Uncle Dolphus's crickets.

Once she looked down to see Esme standing in her backyard on the very edge of Australia waving up at her. All around her, dolphins were popping out of the sea, smiling friendly dolphin smiles.

Soon she was so high the earth looked like a beautiful, blue bubble below her.

Tilly knew when she was getting near the place where the sky hole was, because there was a wrong feeling in the air, like walking up a forgotten path to a house that's been left empty too long. The closer Tilly got, the louder the wrong feeling became; like when Sophie got angry with her clarinet. It wasn't just an out-of-tune feeling though, it was a sad, sore one.

Then she said, 'Oh poor sky,' because now she saw how hurt it was.

And she reached out very gently to touch the

hurting place in the sky. It felt as soft as baby Maya's skin.

'I think you're beautiful anyway,' said Tilly, her eyes prickling.

But the sky winced away from her, the way Tilly did when she cut her knee and Mum put antiseptic on.

And there were so many holes. Not just one, as Tilly'd thought. But hundreds and hundreds . . . There were just too many. Tilly started to cry. How could people be so mean? Didn't they know that once all their atoms used to belong to a star? Maybe they'd forgotten how starry they still were inside. Maybe that was the problem.

But Tilly knew. She knew that, unless humans took proper care of their world, every living creature was going to get hurt, just like the sky was now. And everything in the world was alive. Tilly knew that too.

So that meant Tilly had to do something.

'Don't worry, sky,' Tilly said fiercely. 'I'm here now.'

Her jar felt terribly heavy. Somehow on her flight through the sky it had grown bigger without

Tilly noticing. It was like one of Ali Baba's oil jars in the fairytale book now.

Something amazing had happened to The Cure For Everything as well. It was blue! It was bluer than Ben's butterfly crown and brighter than moonlight, almost too bright to look at, like something that had once lived inside a star.

Tilly dipped a finger in her jar. A smiley feeling started in her fingertip and spread fizzily through her body.

'Our experiment works,' Tilly whispered. 'Wait till I tell Emily.'

'I'm here, silly,' said someone pulling her nightie sleeve, laughing. 'I heard the moon chimes, so there, Tilly Beany.'

'You're in the sky, Em!' said Tilly amazed.

'So's Beth and Nessa,' said Emily. 'And Ben promised not to shout if I let him come too.'

'You're wearing your butterfly hat, Ben,' said Tilly giggling.

'I love it, zat's why,' said Ben shyly.

All the children had Ali Baba jars now.

Beth shook her raggedy fringe out of her eyes. 'Let's get busy,' she said.

'I was going to say that, wasn't I?' said Nessa.

Tilly dipped her fingers in her jar and stroked

them across the torn edges of
the nearest hole in the
sky, as tenderly as if
she was stroking
Maya's cheek.

The moon
chimes became
clearer and
more peaceful.
The smiley feeling
inside Tilly grew
almost too big
to bear.

And far below on
earth, the people made a
soft sighing sound, as
though somehow Tilly was
mending a piece of them too.

And the hole in the
sky was gone.

Tilly looked at her
dazzling fingers in amazement. But
there was no time to lose. 'Soon this dream
will be finished, everybody, and we might not be
able to get back into it,' said Tilly.

'Boy, we'd better work hard,' said Emily.

By the time morning turned the edges of the clouds to gold, every single hole in the sky was mended. The children couldn't see even one tiny wrinkle where the holes used to be. That's how hard Tilly and her friends worked.

And all the time Tilly knew she was dreaming. She knew she was going to wake any minute and find herself in her own bed in her own room.

But she didn't mind; she didn't mind one bit. Because since the butterfly birthday party, Tilly knew for sure that dreams are just a different kind of real to the ordinary kind and that sometimes children's dreams can come true.

They really can.

Welcome to Tilly's
world of rainbows
and wishes
that come true.

The Real
Tilly Beany

"This made us laugh out loud . . .
Really refreshing."

Carnegie Judges

It's boring being ordinary Tilly Beany. There are too many other people Tilly has to be – like Windstar, Jellybear or Matilda Seaflower.

But it's hard on the rest of the family. When they find Cindertilly scrubbing the doorstep, things have really got out of hand!

mammoth

Tilly Beany
and the Best Friend Machine

Tilly Beany has never thought about having a best friend.
But, suddenly, everyone has one.
Only Tilly is alone.

Will Tilly ever find that very special friend who will like her best of all?

mammoth